FUN WiTH BUDDY + LiSA

FUN WITH BUDDY + LISA

FANTAGRAPHICS BOOKS

7563 Lake City Way NE
Seattle, Wa 98115

Editorial co-ordination by Kim Thompson
Design and art direction by Patrick Moriarity
Computer Color by Rebecca Bowen
Published by Gary Groth and Kim Thompson

First Fantagraphics Books edition: April, 1995

ISBN (soft) 1-56097-175-4
ISBN (hard) 1-56097-176-2

• C O N T E N T S •

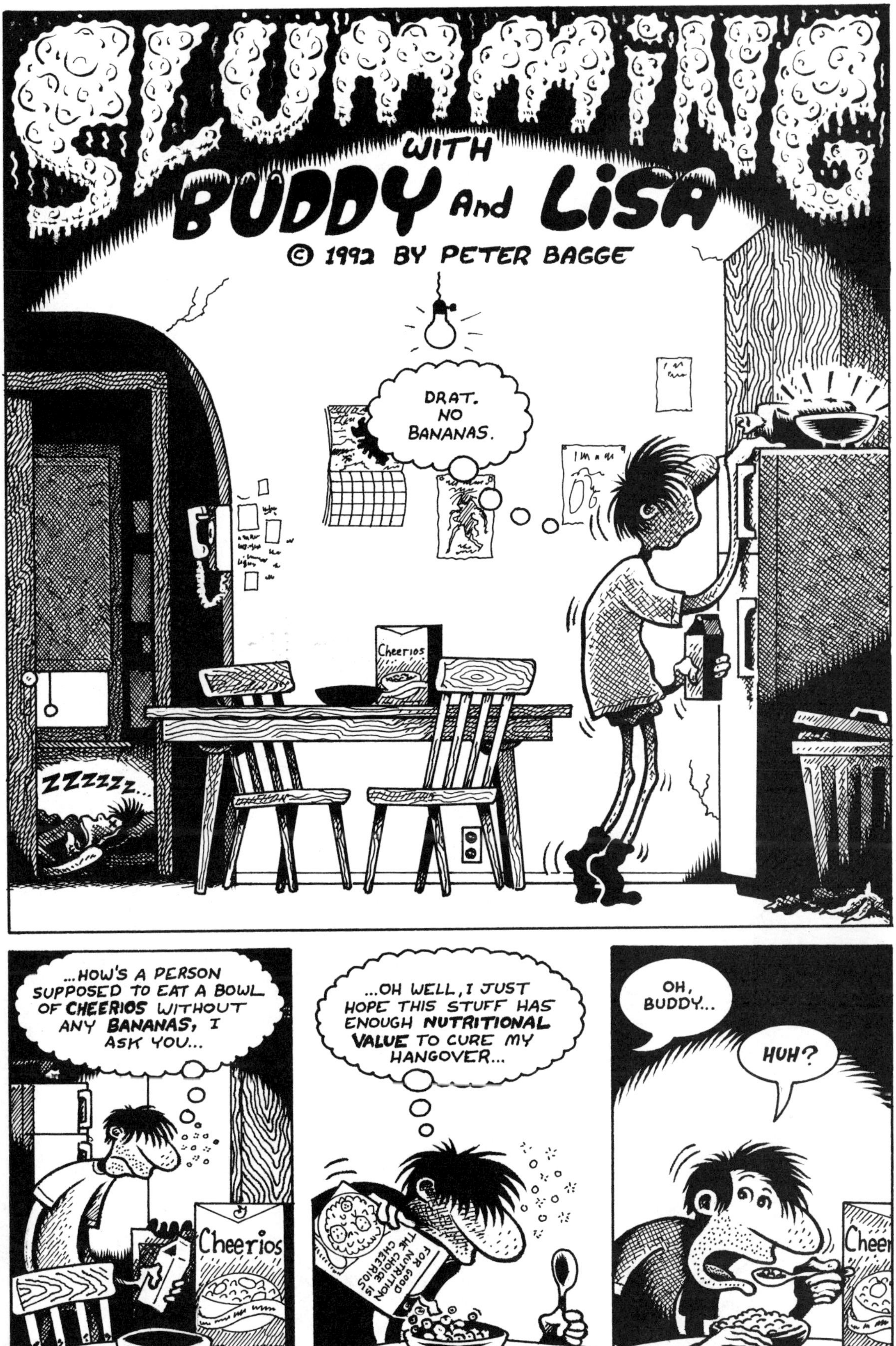

SLUMMING

WITH BUDDY AND LISA

© 1992 BY PETER BAGGE

1

WHAT'S WITH THE SUITCASE, GEORGE? HEADING FOR PEBBLE BEACH?
...I GUESS I SHOULD'VE BROUGHT THIS UP SOONER, BUT I'VE DECIDED TO MOVE OUT...
I'LL BE STAYING WITH MY FOLKS 'TIL I FIND A NEW PLACE...

I-I DON'T GET IT. WHAT BROUGHT THIS ON ALL OF THE SUDDEN?
IN A NUTSHELL, IT'S LISA. EVER SINCE SHE'S BEEN HERE I HAVEN'T HAD A MOMENT'S PEACE. SHE'S UP AT ALL HOURS, LAUGHING, SCREAMING, BLARING MUSIC...
...PLUS THE TWO OF YOU ARE CONSTANTLY FIGHTING...

YEAH, BUT IT'S ONLY TEMPORARY! AS SOON AS SHE FINDS A JOB SHE'LL BE GONE! YOU KNEW THAT WAS THE DEAL!
ALL I KNOW IS THAT SHE'S BEEN HERE FOR THREE MONTHS ALREADY AND IS LOOKING MORE PERMANENT ALL THE TIME...
MEANWHILE MY NERVES ARE TOTALLY SHOT...
I THOUGHT STINKY WAS BAD, BUT SHE TAKES THE CAKE!

WAIT, GEORGE! LET'S NOT BE HASTY! MAYBE WE CAN WORK SOMETHING OUT...
FORGET IT...THERE'S NOTHING LEFT TO BE SAID...
EXCEPT FOR MAYBE ONE THING...
WHAT'S THAT?

...EVER SINCE YOU HOOKED UP WITH THAT WOMAN YOU'VE BEEN GOING DOWNHILL...
...YOU DRINK MORE THAN EVER, AND YOU LOOK LIKE SHIT...
SO WHAT'S YOUR POINT?

MY POINT IS THAT MAYBE YOU SHOULD CONSIDER MOVING OUT TOO, BEFORE IT'S TOO LATE...
OH YEAH? AND WHAT THE HELL IS THAT SUPPOSED TO MEAN? I—

I'LL BE BACK TOMORROW FOR THE REST OF MY THINGS...
HEY, WAIT! WHY DON'T WE SIT DOWN WITH A CUP OF JOE AND TALK THIS OVER, MAN TO—
SLAM!
—MAN.

GRRRRR....

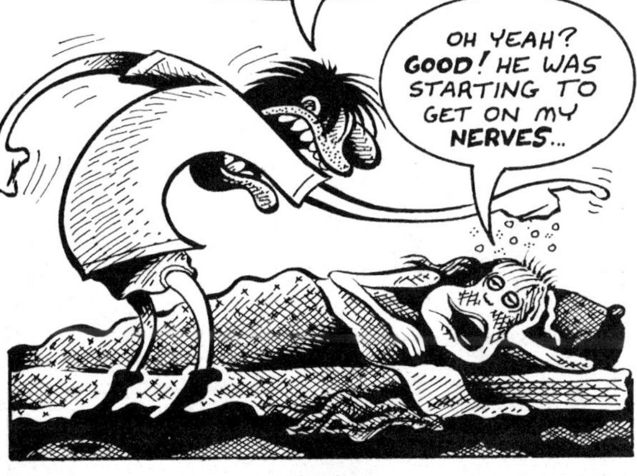

* SEE HATE #10 IF YOU DON'T REMEMBER EITHER.

I HATE TO TELL YOU THIS, LISA, BUT THAT OL' GUILT TRIP AIN'T GONNA WORK ANYMORE...
WHATEVER I OWE YOU I'VE ALREADY PAID YOU BACK IN SPADES...
YEAH, WELL, THAT'S YOUR PROBLEM... I'M GOING BACK TO SLEEP...

NO, IT'S YOUR PROBLEM!
FROM NOW ON THINGS ARE GONNA CHANGE AROUND HERE!
ACK!

FOR ONE THING THERE'LL BE NO MORE OF THIS WAKING UP AT THREE P.M. BULLSHIT!
SHOW SOME SELF-DISCIPLINE, FOR GOD'S SAKE...
YEAH, RIGHT...
PICK, PICK...

...AND FOR ANOTHER THING, I WANT YOU TO START WORKING ON YOUR PHYSICAL APPEARANCE!
YOU LOOK LIKE HELL THESE DAYS!
WHAT ARE YOU TALKING ABOUT? WHAT'S WRONG WITH MY APPEARANCE?
ITCH, ITCH

WHAT'S WRONG?! HOW ABOUT THOSE HAIRY ARMPITS OF YOURS! THEY'RE DISGUSTING!
OH-HO! SO NOW HE SHOWS HIS TRUE COLORS! "MR. ENLIGHTENED" IS JUST ANOTHER CHAUVINIST PIG!
WHY DON'T YOU SHAVE YOUR PITS, IF YOU THINK IT'S SO WONDERFUL!

BECAUSE I DON'T WANT TO FUCK SOMEONE THAT LOOKS LIKE ME, THAT'S WHY!
...I WANT A GIRLFRIEND WHO AT LEAST MAKES AN ATTEMPT TO LOOK PRETTY, FOR CRYIN' OUT LOUD...
GASP

SO SAVE ALL THAT FEMINIST CRAP FOR SOMEONE ELSE! GO FIND YOURSELF SOME WIMPY, SISSY FINE ARTS MAJOR WHO'LL TELL YOU THAT YOUR GRISLY BODY HAIR IS A BEAUTIFUL THING WHILE HE SECRETLY JERKS OFF TO LINGERIE ADS BUT DON'T EXPECT ME TO LIKE IT!

SLAM!
SNIFF

STOMP!
STOMP!
STOMP!

NOW MAYBE I CAN EAT MY BREAKFAST IN PEACE...
Cheer

Cheer

PLOP!

Cheer

OH MY GOD, WHAT HAVE I DONE?
HOW COULD I BE SO HEARTLESS AND CRUEL?
Cheer

I WOULDN'T BE AT ALL SURPRISED IF SHE JUST GOT UP AND LEFT ME...
THAT SEEMS TO BE THE THEME FOR TODAY, ANYWAY...

IN FACT, THAT'S THE STORY OF MY LIFE...EVERYONE RUNS AWAY FROM ME SOONER OR LATER...
I'M SUCH AN ASSHOLE...
Cheer

HEY, WHAT IS THIS WITH THE SELF-PITY ROUTINE?
...WHAT I DID JUST NOW WAS RIGHT-ON, NOT TO MENTION LONG OVERDUE...
Cheer

IT'S ABOUT TIME I PUT MY FOOT DOWN WITH HER! SHE'LL BE BETTER OFF FOR IT!
AND SHE'LL PROBABLY SHOW MORE RESPECT FOR ME, TOO
SHOVEL!

...NO DOUBT ABOUT IT, WOMEN ADMIRE A MAN WHO KNOWS HOW TO TREAT A WOMAN WITH A FIRM HAND...
GOODBYE, BUDDY...

HEY! WHERE ARE YOU GOING?!
OUT. WHAT DO YOU CARE?

YOU'RE NOT LEAVING FOR GOOD, ARE YOU? IF IT'S ABOUT WHAT I SAID I REALLY DIDN'T MEAN IT...
YES YOU DID, AND LET ME GO...
I'LL BE BACK LATER...

B-B-BUT WHERE ARE YOU GOING? WHEN WILL YOU BE BACK? DO YOU WANT ME TO GO WITH YOU, OR...
ENOUGH WITH THE 3RD DEGREE, OKAY? I'LL BE BACK WHEN I'LL BE BACK! NOW LEAVE ME ALONE!

SLAM!

WELL! HOW DO YOU LIKE THAT!
THE LITTLE WENCH IS AS INSOLENT AS EVER...
SO MUCH FOR MY "STRAIGHTENING HER OUT..."

SO NOW WHAT? DO I SIT HERE AND ACCEPT THINGS AS THEY ARE, OR DO I ACT LIKE A MAN AND DO SOMETHING ABOUT IT?

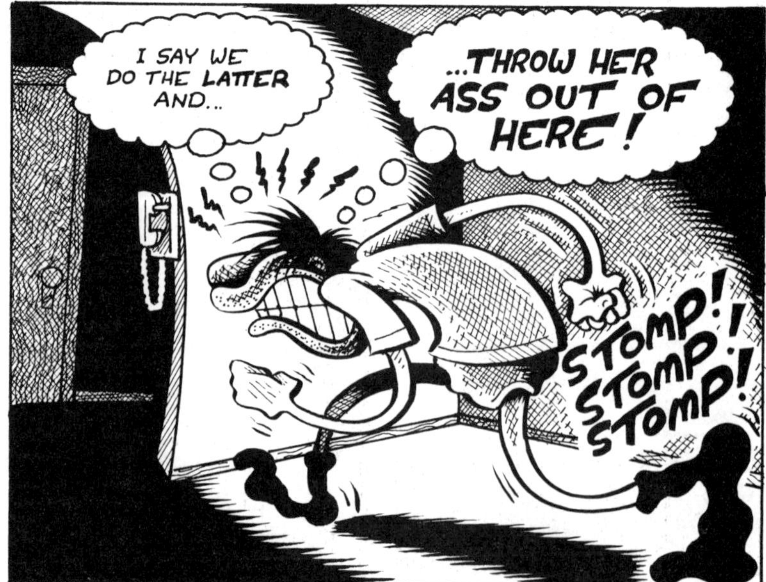

I SAY WE DO THE LATTER AND...
...THROW HER ASS OUT OF HERE!
STOMP! STOMP! STOMP!

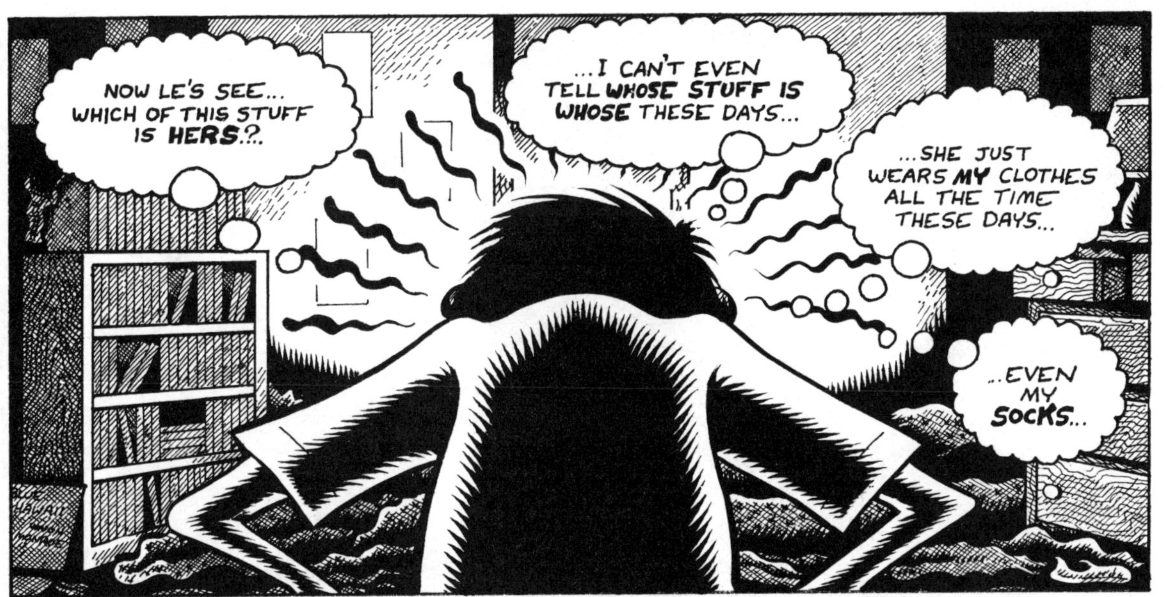

NOW LE'S SEE... WHICH OF THIS STUFF IS HERS.?..
...I CAN'T EVEN TELL WHOSE STUFF IS WHOSE THESE DAYS...
...SHE JUST WEARS MY CLOTHES ALL THE TIME THESE DAYS...
...EVEN MY SOCKS...

...MAYBE SHE SHOVED HER OWN THINGS UNDERNEATH SOMETHING...

OH MAN, WILL YOU LOOK AT THIS! HER PERIOD BLOOD STAIN HAS SOAKED CLEAR THROUGH TO THE OTHER SIDE OF THE MATTRESS!
DISGUSTING!

MAN, WHAT A GROSS, SLOBBY CHICK LISA IS...
...I DON'T RE-MEMBER VALERIE PUKING AND FARTING AND BLEEDING ALL OVER THE PLACE...
...VALERIE WAS THE WAY A WOMAN SHOULD BE...
...SHE WAS NON-HUMAN!
KICK!

AAH, FUCK THIS!
I'M TOO TIRED TO WADE THROUGH ALL OF THIS JUNK...
...I'LL JUST WAIT FOR HER TO COME HOME AND MAKE HER DO IT!
TOSS!

...I'LL JUST SIT RIGHT HERE, MAKE MYSELF COMFORTABLE, AND WHEN SHE COMES HOME I'LL HAND HER HER WALKING PAPERS...

I CAN WAIT... I'VE GOT ALL DAY... I... ...I...

...ZZZZZ...

THREE HOURS LATER...
SLAM!
OH, BUDDY! I'M HOME!
ZZZZZORK! HUH? WHOOZAT?

OH, LISA, I—
BOING!
HOW DO YOU LIKE MY NEW OUTFIT? I GOT MOST OF IT SECOND-HAND...

I HAD MY HAIR FIXED, AND MY NAILS DONE, TOO...
I SPENT ALMOST ALL THAT WAS LEFT OF MY MONEY, SO I HOPE YOU THINK IT WAS WORTH IT...
...A HUMMINA HUMMINA HUMMINA...

...Y'KNOW, MUCH OF WHAT YOU SAID WAS TRUE—I HAVE BEEN LETTING MYSELF GO TO SEED LATELY, AND THAT HASN'T BEEN GOOD FOR MY MORALE...
YEAH, YEAH—WHO CARES? ENOUGH TALK! LET'S GIVE THIS NEW GET-UP OF YOURS A TEST SPIN, SHALL WE?

NOT SO FAST, BUSTER! THERE'S A FEW THINGS I'D LIKE TO GET OFF OF MY CHEST AS WELL!
OOF!
SHOVE!

AW JEEZ, LISA, CAN'T IT WAIT? RIGHT NOW I JUST WANT TO LOOK AT YOU IN YOUR NEW THREADS...
HEY! LOOK WITH YOUR EYES, NOT WITH YOUR HANDS, YOU DIRTY LITTLE...
FEEL! GROPE!

ZOOM!
TEE-HEE!
HEY! WHERE ARE YOU...
OHHH, THE BEDROOM, EH? I GET IT...
ZIP!

SLAM!
CLICK!
?!? WHAT'S THE BIG IDEA?!
OPEN UP!
NO! NOT UNTIL YOU LISTEN TO WHAT I HAVE TO SAY!

...NOW, I'M BIG ENOUGH TO ADMIT THAT I'VE BEEN NEGLECTING MYSELF, AND AS YOU CAN SEE I DID SOMETHING ABOUT IT...
BONK!
ARRRRGH...

...BUT YOU CAN'T DENY THAT YOU'VE BEEN JUST AS BAD LATELY IN THE PERSONAL HYGIENE DEPARTMENT, AND THAT THESE MATTERS OF... AESTHETICS... MEAN JUST AS MUCH TO US GIRLS AS IT DOES TO YOU...
SSSSSSSLIDE...

...SO I DON'T THINK IT'S ASKING TOO MUCH FOR YOU TO MAKE AN EFFORT TO LOOK NICE ONCE IN A BLUE MOON EITHER...
BUDDY? ARE YOU LISTENING TO ME?
I'M LISTENING! I'M LISTENING! NOW WILL YOU PUL-LEASE COME OUT OF THERE?

DO YOU AGREE WITH WHAT I JUST SAID, OR...
YES! ABSOLUTELY! NOW COME ON OUT SO I CAN SEE YOU!

ALL RIGHT... BUT THERE'LL BE NONE OF THAT GRABBY STUFF, YOU HEAR ME? I WANT YOU TO ACT LIKE A GENTLE-MAN...
YOU'RE ALWAYS IN SUCH A HURRY...
ALL RIGHT, I'LL ACT LIKE A GENTLEMAN! NOW COME OUT HERE!

OKAY, HERE I COME...
TEE-HEE...
CREEEEK...

...BUDDY? ARE YOU THERE?
I DON'T SEE YOU...

...BUDDY?

YEEHAH!
EEEK!

BUDDY, TAKE IT EASY! I TOLD YOU, NOT SO FAST!
...AND DON'T RIP MY BRAND NEW STOCKINGS! I JUST—
SNORT! *SLOBBER!* *GRUNT!*

RRRRRRRRIP!
GODDAMMIT, BUDDY! WILL YOU SLOW DOWN?! I DON'T HAVE MY THING IN, AND...
GRUNT, SNORT...

SHHHHLORK!
OHHH GOD...

...EEEASY, BUDDY... SSSLOW DOWN... WAIT FOR ME...
...DON'T YOU DARE...
...UH, UH, UH, UH, UH, UH, UH, UH, UH, UH, UH, UH—

UNGAWA!!!
...COME.

GOD DAMN YOU, BUDDY! I TOLD YOU TO TAKE IT SLOW!
YOU'RE SO FUCKING SELFISH!
LEAP!
FLOP!

I SWEAR I'LL NEVER GET DRESSED UP FOR YOU AGAIN! WHY SHOULD I BOTHER? WHAT'S THE FUCKING POINT?!
I HATE YOU! I HATE YOU! I HATE YOU!
KICK! KICK! KICK!
OUCH! OUCH! OUCH!

...BOO, HOO, HOO, HOO, HOO HOO!...
OOOOOH... THAT FELT GOOD...

LATER, AND IN SPITE OF EVERYTHING, POST-COITAL HARMONY PREVAILS...

WHATCHA WATCHIN'?
CHECK THIS OUT, LISA! THEY'VE GOT THIS FAT, UGLY, HIGHLY DYSFUNCTIONAL FAMILY ON THE MAURY POVITCH SHOW WHO'VE GOT SO MANY "PROBLEMS" IT'S BEYOND BELIEF!

...THE FATHER'S A BARELY COHERENT ALCOHOLIC-TYPE, AND THE MOTHER'S THIS TEARY-EYED RELIGIOUS NUT WHO'S BEEN "VICTIMIZED" BY EVERYONE AND EVERYTHING...
YOU DON'T HAVE TO TELL ME ABOUT IT. THAT'S MY FAMILY.
...THIS IS VERY HARD FOR ME TO TALK ABOUT, MAURY...
CAT

...HUH? WHAT?! ARE YOU SERIOUS?
I KID YOU NOT. THEY'VE ALREADY BEEN ON ALL THE LOCAL TALK SHOWS...LOOKS LIKE THEY'RE WORKING THEIR WAY UP TO THE "BIG TIME"...
...AIRING OUT THEIR DIRTY LAUNDRY IN PUBLIC HAS BECOME A SECOND CAREER FOR THEM...
SOMETIMES THEY EVEN START TALKING ABOUT ME...

...AND LISA, IF YOU CAN HEAR ME NOW, I URGE YOU TO GIVE UP YOUR PAGANISTIC WAYS AND COME HOME TO US...WE NEED EACH OTHER...
YOU SEE? THERE SHE GOES AGAIN...
THIS IS....UN-REAL...

DROP DEAD, YA OLD PHONEY! I'LL COME HOME WHEN HELL FREEZES OVER AND NOT A MOMENT SOONER!
* BOO-HOO * * SOB *
YIKES!

...I...UH... ALWAYS WONDERED WHY YOU NEVER TALK ABOUT YOUR FAMILY...
SO NOW YOU KNOW...
...LAST TIME I SAW THEM WAS LAST THANKSGIVING...
BIG MISTAKE...
NEVER AGAIN...

RING! RING! RING!
UH-OH, PHONE'S RINGING... I'LL GET IT...
...THEY STILL LIVE IN THE SAME HOUSE I GREW UP IN, OVER IN WEST SEATTLE...
...SOMETIMES I'LL EVEN SEE ONE OF MY COUSINS DRIVE PAST ME OUT ON THE STREET...

...THEY NEVER STOP, OR EVEN HONK THE HORN AND WAVE... THEY ACT LIKE THEY DON'T EVEN KNOW ME...
HELLO?
HELLO? IS THIS A... MR. HAROLD BRADLEY?

YES...
MR. BRADLEY, WE'RE CONDUCTING A POLL ON BEHALF OF A NATIONAL NEWS ORGANIZATION...DO YOU ACT AS THE SPOKES-PERSON FOR THIS HOUSEHOLD?
ITCH! ITCH!

I MOST CERTAINLY DO!
FINE, THEN IF YOU HAVE THE TIME I'D LIKE TO ASK YOU A FEW QUESTIONS...
FIRST OFF, HOW OLD ARE YOU?

UH... 24.
OKAY... AND WHICH OF THE FOLLOWING DOES YOUR HOUSEHOLD INCOME FALL UNDER: (A) BELOW $20,000, (B) $20-35,000, (C) $35-60,000, OR (D) OVER $60,000...

UMMM... THE LAST ONE...
OVER $60,000?
YEAH...
OHHH-KAY...

NOW, LET ME ASK YOU THIS: ARE YOU SATISFIED THAT YOUR GENERATION WILL BE BETTER OFF FINANCIALLY THAN YOUR PARENTS' GENERATION? THAT IS TO SAY...
WAIT A MINUTE— WHAT DO YOU MEAN BY "SATISFIED"?

..HOW CAN ANYONE BE "SATISFIED" WITH THE FUTURE?
I, UH-HA-HA!— ADMIT THAT THE WORDING IS A BIT AWKWARD, BUT WE JUST WANT TO GET A READING ON HOW PEOPLE ARE—
OKAY, OKAY, PUT ME DOWN AS "SATISFIED".

WOULD THAT BE: (A) VERY SATISFIED, (B) SOMEWHAT SATISFIED, (C) UN-SATISFIED, OR...
MAKE THAT VERY SATISFIED...
ALL RIGHT... AS A 24-YEAR-OLD MAKING OVER 60 GRAND PER, I CAN UNDERSTAND YOUR OPTI-MISM...

BWAAAH!
UH-OH... LOOK, I, UH, GOTTA GO...
BUT, YOU ONLY ANSWERED THREE QUESTIONS, AND...

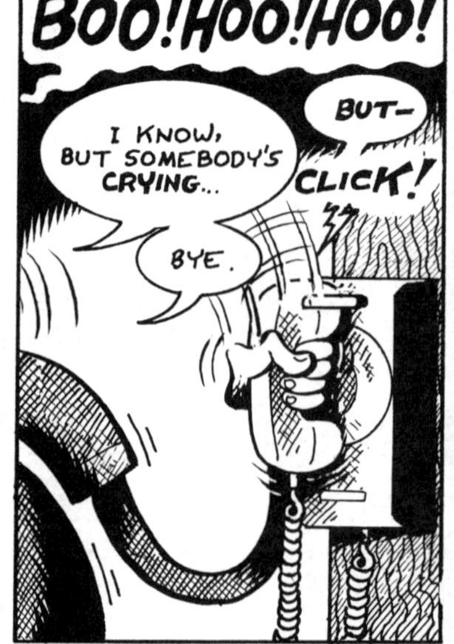

BOO! HOO! HOO!
I KNOW, BUT SOMEBODY'S CRYING...
BUT—
CLICK!
BYE.

LISA? WHAT'S THE MATTER?
NOTHING... *SNIFF*...NEVER MIND...

NO, REALLY, YOU CAN TELL ME...
OH...*SNIFF*...YOU'LL PROBABLY THINK I'M BEING SILLY, BUT THE REASON I'M CRYING IS BECAUSE...BECAUSE...

...THERE'S NO BANANAS FOR MY CHEERIOS! BWAAAAAAHHH!
OH...

...I THOUGHT MAYBE YOU WERE UPSET OVER SEEING YOUR FAMILY ON T.V...
MY FAMILY?! FUCK MY FAMILY!
LIKE I COULD GIVE TWO SHITS ABOUT THOSE ASSHOLES!

UNGH!
SPLAT!

FUME...
PLOP!

...BUDDY?
YES?

...EEEEYES, WE HAVE NO BANANAS, WE HAVE NO BANANAS TODAY!...

...GET IT? HAHAHAHA HAHAHA HAHA...
GOT IT.

THAT NIGHT...

THAT BATH LOOKS GOOD...
UM-HMMM... I HAVEN'T TAKEN ONE IN SOOOO LONG...

MAKE ROOM, 'CUZ I'M COMING IN, TOO...
YOU'RE DRUNK, AREN'T YOU? I HATE IT WHEN YOU GET DRUNK WITHOUT ME...

WHAT ARE YOU TALKING ABOUT? I SAW YOU SUCKIN' DOWN SOME BREWSKIES EARLIER...
YES, BUT YOU DRANK A LOT MORE THAN ME SINCE THEN! I LIKE THE TWO OF US TO BE THE SAME AMOUNT DRUNK!
THESE THINGS ARE IMPORTANT TO ME...

MMMMM... I CAN FEEL YOUR TITTIES WITH MY FEET...
SAY, WHEN WAS THE LAST TIME WE PORKED?
WHEN?! DON'T YOU REMEMBER THIS AFTERNOON?!

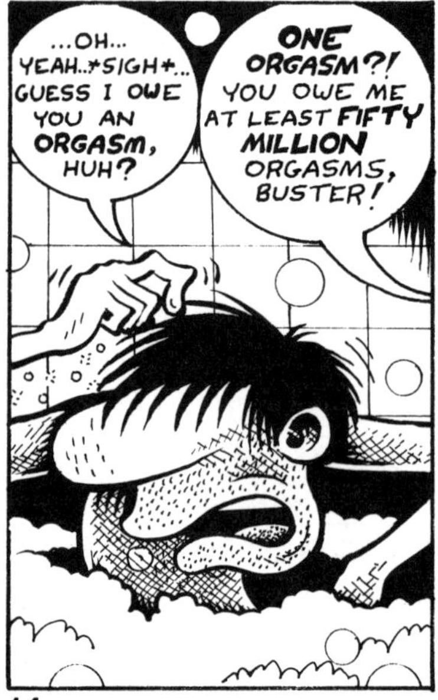
...OH... YEAH...*SIGH*... GUESS I OWE YOU AN ORGASM, HUH?
ONE ORGASM?! YOU OWE ME AT LEAST FIFTY MILLION ORGASMS, BUSTER!

FIFTY MILLION, EH? IS THAT ALL?
..WELL, MAYBE I CAN START PAYING YOU BACK RIGHT NOW...
OH, YEAH, RIGHT...

I'M SERIOUS... I LIKE THE WAY YOUR SKIN TURNS BEET RED FROM THE HOT WATER...
IT MAKES ME HORNY...
WHO DO YOU THINK YOU'RE FOOLING? YOU'RE TOO DRUNK TO GET A HARD ON!

...UMPF! ...JUST SIT BACK AND ENJOY THE RIDE, BABY...
HA! JUST AS I SUSPECTED! YOUR DICK IS TOTALLY LIMP!

...EWWW, AND YOUR WHOLE BODY FEELS COLD AND CLAMMY! DON'T YOU HAVE ANY CIRCULATION LEFT?
FEH... CIRCULATION... WHO NEEDS IT...
BURP!

UGH! GET OFFA ME, YA BIG LUMMOX! YER SQUASHIN' ME!
URRRGH... SHITTR...
...HEY, LISA...
SPLASH! SPLOSH!

SIGH... WHAT?
...UH...I... ...I THINK I MIGHT BE AN ALCOHOLIC...
URP!

NO SHIT, SHERLOCK! NOW GET OFF OF ME!
UMPF!
UMPF!
URRRRGH...
SPLASH! SPLOOSH!

SIGH I GIVE UP...
...ZZZZZZz...

?!?...
BUDDY? I THINK WE'RE SINKING...
BUDDY? CAN YOU HEAR ME?
ZZZZZz...

BUDDY! BUDDYBLUBBB BLUBBLBLrrr...
ZZZZZz...

BLURBL BLUBBLY BLBBLUB...
?!? WHERE'S THAT BUBBLY SOUND COMING FROM?

OMIGOD!

LISA! ARE YOU ALL RIGHT?! TALK TO ME!
KOFF *SPUTTER* *GAG*
SPLOSH!!

HERE, I'LL LAY YOU DOWN ON THE FLOOR AND PERFORM THE HEIMLICH MANEUVER ON YOU!
GAG *CHOKE* *WHEEZE*

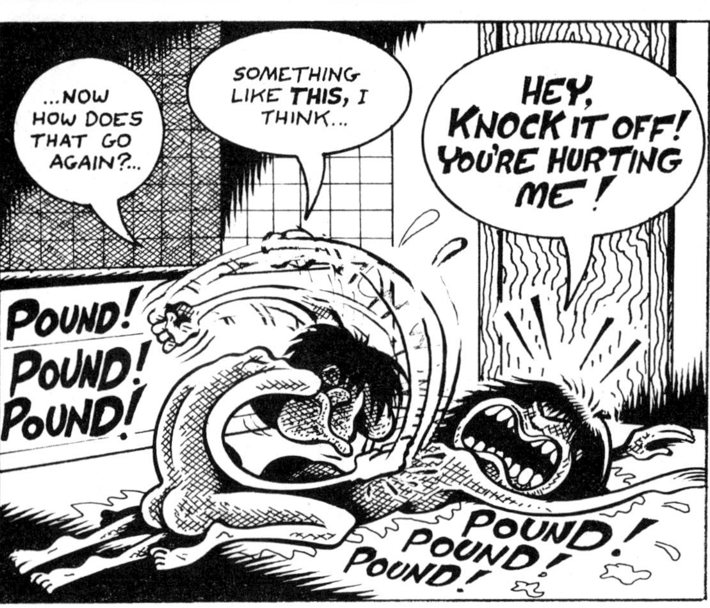

...NOW HOW DOES THAT GO AGAIN?...
SOMETHING LIKE THIS, I THINK...
HEY, KNOCK IT OFF! YOU'RE HURTING ME!
POUND! POUND! POUND!
POUND! POUND! POUND!

LISA! YOU'RE ALIVE! YOU'RE ALIVE! OH, THANK GOD IN HEAVEN!
EWWW, CALM DOWN, WILL YOU? YER GIVIN' ME THE CREEPS!

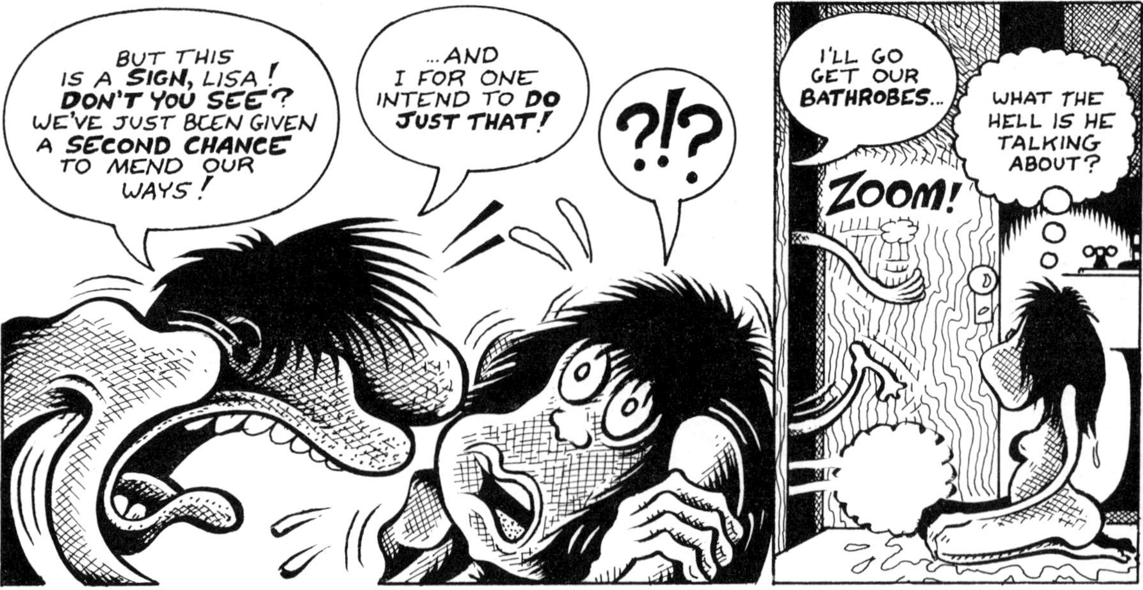

BUT THIS IS A SIGN, LISA! DON'T YOU SEE? WE'VE JUST BEEN GIVEN A SECOND CHANCE TO MEND OUR WAYS!
...AND I FOR ONE INTEND TO DO JUST THAT!
?!?
I'LL GO GET OUR BATHROBES...
WHAT THE HELL IS HE TALKING ABOUT?
ZOOM!

FIFTEEN MINUTES LATER...

YOU MADE COFFEE?
UH-HUH... TRYING TO SOBER UP...
HELP YOURSELF IF YOU WANT SOME...

SIP

...OH MY, BUDDY! YOU'RE SHAKING LIKE A LEAF! ARE YOU OKAY?

OH GOD, LISA! I ALMOST KILLED YOU! I'M SUCH A DRUNKEN, SELFISH, THOUGHTLESS, DESPICABLE FOOL! I CAN HARDLY STAND MYSELF!
THERE, THERE...
PAT! PAT!

...DON'T TORTURE YOURSELF, BUDDY... IT WAS NO BIG DEAL...
"NO BIG DEAL"?! YOU COULD'VE DROWNED! DON'T YOU HATE ME BECAUSE OF THAT?

NAH... IN FACT I THOUGHT IT WAS KINDA COOL... I NEVER CAME SO CLOSE TO DEATH BEFORE... IT WAS SORT OF EXCITING...
EXCITING?!? HOW COULD YOU CALL SUCH A PATHETIC INCIDENT "EXCITING"?

LOOK AT US, LISA! WE'RE PITIFUL! WE'VE GOTTA START CLEANING UP OUR ACT RIGHT NOW, 'CUZ WE'RE ON THE FAST TRACK TO NOWHERE!
SO WHAT DO YOU PROPOSE WE DO ABOUT IT?

WELL, THE FIRST THING WE OUGHT TO DO IS CALL UP ONE OF THOSE TECHNICAL SCHOOLS THAT TEACH YOU HOW TO WORK WITH COMPUTERS, 'CUZ COMPUTERS ARE THE KEY TO THE FUTURE, AND WE'VE GOT TO PUT AN END TO THIS HAND-TO-MOUTH EXISTENCE WE'VE BEEN LEADING...
?
POUND!

...BECAUSE I FOR ONE DON'T WANT TO BE LIVING IN A SHITHOLE LIKE THIS WHEN I'M SIXTY, DO YOU?
NO, BUT... COMPUTERS? YUCK!

HAVE A SATISFYING FUTURE! —P.B.

LEONARD the LOVE GOD

MEETS "DAME DARCY," BY P. BAGGE © 1992

A DAY IN THE LIFE OF...
COLLECTOR SCUM!
STARRING "BUDDY BRADLEY" BY PETER BAGGE ©1993
SEA
COM 'R US
PRICE GUIDE
PRICE GUIDE
MAGAZINES
SPIDER MAN
SOX
25¢
25¢
50¢
50¢
50¢
MAN, THIS SUCKS! WE HAVEN'T MADE ONE RED CENT YET!
YEAH, WELL, THE WORST PART OF MANNING ONE OF THESE TABLES IS WAITING OUT THE LONG DRY SPELLS...
JUST YOU WAIT, WE'LL PROBABLY MAKE A TON OF MONEY ALL AT ONCE...YOU'LL SEE...
ALL I KNOW IS WE BETTER SELL SOMETHING SOON OR I'LL START CRYING...
...OH LOOK, THERE'S PHIL! MAYBE HE'LL BUY SOMETHING FROM US...
...OH PHIL!
HUH...I DIDN'T KNOW HE CAME TO THESE THINGS...
AND LOOK AT THAT GIRL HE'S WITH... YIKES!

OH, HI, YOU GUYS! I DIDN'T KNOW YOU HAD A TABLE!
...GETTING RID OF SOME OLD, UNWANTED STUFF, BUDDY?
TRYING TO, ANYWAY...
JOE BLOW'S COMIC SHOP

WOW, LISA! YOU LOOK GREAT! ALL DRESSED UP FOR THE CON, HUH?
I GUESS...
TEE-HEE!

OH, THIS IS MY FRIEND IMELDA...
HI! YA WANNA SEE WHAT WE FOUND?
SURE...
"IMELDA"—SHEESH! WHY DO SO MANY WOMEN IN THIS TOWN HAVE FAKE NAMES?

IT'S AN OLD PARTRIDGE FAMILY COMIC BOOK! CAN YOU DIG IT?
...SOMEONE DREW SEX ORGANS ALL OVER IT, SO WE GOT IT FOR ONLY 25 CENTS!
PARTRIDGE FAMILY
...IF YOU ASK ME IT'S AN IMPROVEMENT...
VERY IMPRESSIVE...

...OH, WOW! YOU'VE GOT OLD TIGER BEAT MAGAZINES!
COOL... DO YOU HAVE ANY FROM, LIKE, THE EARLY TO MID-SEVENTIES?
A FEW, THOUGH MOST OF THESE ARE FROM THE LATE SIXTIES...

HERE, I'LL TAKE THIS ONE... I LIKE TO BEAT OFF TO PICTURES OF ERIC ESTRADA...
OOH, AND THIS ONE HAS THE BRADY BUNCH FROM THEIR "HIPPY" PERIOD...
THE SEVENTIES, LIKE, TOTALLY FUCKING RULE, MAN!
HOW MUCH?
THOSE ARE TWO BUCKS EACH...

THEY'RE A BARGAIN AT ANY PRICE...
WE'RE GONNA POKE AROUND A BIT MORE, AND IF WE HAVE ANY MONEY LEFT WE'LL BE BACK FOR THE REST OF THOSE MAGAZINES...
BYE, PHIL!
SEE YA!
LATER...

HMMM... I WONDER IF THAT "IMELDA" BROAD IS PHIL'S GIRLFRIEND...
IF SHE IS I HATE HER...
?!? WHAT?!? OH, GET REAL, LISA! DIDN'T YOU JUST HEAR HIM SAY HE LIKES TO SPILL HIS JUICE OVER ERIC ESTRADA?

SO? THAT DOESN'T NECESSARILY MEAN ANYTHING...
HEY, WHAT IS THIS? I THOUGHT I WAS YOUR BOYFRIEND! WHAT ARE YOU PINING AFTER THAT GUY FOR?

OH, LEAVE ME ALONE! I CAN INDULGE IN MY OWN HARMLESS LITTLE FANTASIES IF I WANT TO!
WHAT'S IT TO YOU, ANYWAY? IT'S NO SKIN OFF YOUR NOSE...
OKAY! OKAY! YEESH!

* SIGH *... DID YOU NOTICE HOW SICKLY AND EMACIATED LOOKING PHIL HAS BECOME?
...HE JUST GETS MORE BEAUTIFUL ALL THE TIME...
I-YI-YI...

...'SCUSE ME, LADY, BUT HOW MUCH FOR THIS COMPLETE SET OF "DINOSAUR ATTACK" CARDS?
HUH? OH, I DON'T KNOW...
THOSE ARE $150.00.

ONE HUNDRED AND FIFTY DOLLARS?!?!? THAT'S A LOT OF MONEY...
IT'S A COMPLETE SET, KID...YOU'D BE LUCKY TO FIND THAT AT ANY PRICE...

YEAH, BUT I DON'T HAVE $150.00... I'M JUST A HIGH SCHOOL KID!
...I THOUGHT THEY'D BE MORE LIKE FIFTY DOLLARS...
ONE FIFTY. TAKE IT OR LEAVE IT.

* SIGH *...
YEAH... LET'S GO...
...PSST... ...PSST... ...PSST...
?!?

, BUDDY, WHAT'S WRONG WITH YOU? FIFTY DOLLARS IS A LOT OF MONEY...
I KNOW, I KNOW...
...LOOK, I'M GONNA STEP OUTSIDE FOR A SMOKE, AND WHILE I'M GONE I WANT YOU TO OFFER THOSE CARDS TO THOSE KIDS FOR $100...

BUT THEY'RE NOT COMING BACK! YOU JUST—
BELIEVE ME, THEY'LL BE BACK, ONCE THEY SEE THAT THE "MEAN MAN" HAS GONE AWAY...
AS LONG AS YOU ACT LIKE YOU'RE DOING THEM A BIG FAVOR THEY'LL BE MORE THAN HAPPY TO FORK OVER THE DOUGH...

I DON'T KNOW...$100 IS A LOT TO ASK FROM A KID...
HEY, ANY 16-YEAR-OLD WHO'S READY TO BLOW EVEN $50.00 ON JUNK LIKE THIS OBVIOUSLY HAS MONEY TO BURN...
DON'T WASTE YOUR TIME PITYING THOSE SPOILED BRATS!
COOL!
GRRRRR..
...WHAT DOES THIS THING DO?

WELL... OKAY... IF YOU THINK IT WILL WORK...
I KNOW IT'LL WORK! WHY DO YOU THINK I ASKED YOU TO GET ALL DOLLED UP FOR THIS THING? IT'S BECAUSE THESE NERDS NEVER HAGGLE OVER PRICES WITH A GIRL IN A MINI-SKIRT!
THEY'RE TOO THRILLED THAT YOU'RE EVEN TALKING TO 'EM!

...JUST LOOK AT THOSE GUYS OVER THERE, LINING UP TO HAVE THEIR PICTURE TAKEN WITH "INTERGALACTIC LASS"...
...AND THEN THEY SHEEPISHLY BUY MULTIPLE COPIES OF THE COMIC BOOK SHE'S PROMOTING, EVEN IF IT'S A TOTAL PIECE OF SHIT!
INTERGA LASS
IN PER

SHE MUST BE FREEZING IN THAT OUTFIT...
YEAH, WELL, THAT'S HER PROBLEM...
YOU WANT ME TO GET YOU SOME COFFEE OR SOMETHING?

NAH.
SUIT YERSELF...
...AND REMEMBER WHAT I SAID!

FIVE MINUTES LATER...

...PSST, PSST...
UH-HUH...
OH MY! THEY'RE HEADING BACK HERE ALREADY! I GUESS BUDDY WAS RIGHT!
...'SCUSE ME, LADY, I, UMMM... HOW MUCH FOR THESE BACK ISSUES OF FANGORIA?...
I DUNNO, BUT HEY! IF YOU'RE STILL INTERESTED IN THOSE DINOSAUR CARDS I'LL LET YOU HAVE THEM FOR ONLY $100!

R-REALLY?
SURE! I KNOW MY FRIEND WANTED $150.00 FOR 'EM, BUT I THINK THAT'S TOO MUCH TO ASK FROM A HIGHSCHOOLER, SO I'M OFFERING YOU A "STUDENT DISCOUNT"!
I HOPE THEY CAN SEE MY LEGS FROM OVER THERE...
...WISH I WASN'T SO GODDAMNED SHORT!

...PSST, PSST, PSST...
HMMM...

OKAY. I'LL TAKE IT!
REALLY? I MEAN, SWELL!

WOW, THAT WAS EASY! I GUESS BUDDY KNEW WHAT HE WAS TALKING ABOUT!
...NOW I ALMOST FEEL GUILTY FOR TAKING ADVANTAGE OF THEIR SEXUAL TIMIDITY, BUT WHAT THE HECK—A GAL'S GOTTA MAKE A BUCK!
PSST, PSST...
DMAN

...WHAT'S THIS? HE'S COMING BACK AGAIN!...
...HOPEFULLY TO COUGH UP SOME MORE DOUGH...
TEE-HEE!

HELLO, AGAIN! IS THERE SOMETHING ELSE THAT YOU'RE INTERESTED IN?
N-NO, IT'S JUST THAT MY FRIEND WANTED ME TO TELL YOU THAT HE... THAT HE...
YES?

...WANTS TO BONE YOU UP THE BUTT!

GOOD LORD! HOW FUCKED-UP CAN YOU GET?!
TEE-HEE!
SNICKER!
CHORTLE!
SNORT!
?

...WELL I'LL BE... BUDDY BRADLEY'S MOVING UP IN THE WORLD BY RENTING HIS OWN TABLE, I SEE...
HUH? HOW DID YOU KNOW THIS WAS BUDDY'S—

BECAUSE I RECOGNIZE HIS STUFF. I'M THE ONE WHO SOLD HIM HALF OF THIS JUNK...
MY NAME'S YAHTZI...I'VE GOT A BOOTH IN THE NEXT ISLE...
HERE'S MY CARD...
HI, I'M —

...SO BUDDY'S ASKING $10.00 EACH FOR THESE OLD ARCADES, EH? WHAT A JOKE...
HERE, I'LL GIVE YOU $25.00 FOR THE WHOLE SET...
BUT, I DON'T...
MAGAZIN

RELAX. IF HE'S GOT HALF A BRAIN HE'LL KNOW HE MADE A GOOD DEAL...
...TELL HIM I SAID HI...
LATER...
BUT, I—I...

SIGH... I WISH I WAS ANYWHERE BUT HERE RIGHT NOW...
MAGAZINES
MAGAZINES

MEANWHILE...
ARTIST ALLEY
BIG SKY
STONED AGAIN
...SO HOW'S IT GOING SO FAR, BUDDY?
NOT SO GOOD. I JUST SPENT EVERYTHING I MADE SO FAR TODAY AT THE CONCESSION STAND...
PUB

YEAH, WELL, I TOLD YOU THIS CAN BE A TOUGH RACKET...
IT TAKES A CERTAIN SKILL, JUST LIKE EVERYTHING ELSE...
OH, I'M NOT READY TO THROW IN THE TOWEL JUST YET...
SO HOW'S BUSINESS BEEN FOR YOU?

HMPF. LIKE I SHOULD TALK...
EVERYONE'S WALKING AROUND WITH THEIR NOSES STUCK IN A PRICE GUIDE, AND SINCE WHAT I SELL ISN'T LISTED IN ANY PRICE GUIDE THEY AVOID ME LIKE THE PLAGUE...
YEAH, WELL, MOST OF WHAT YOU SELL IS BOOKS, AND WHO WANTS BOOKS?
THESE PEOPLE AREN'T LOOKING FOR SOMETHING TO READ...
DAD, I'M BORED...
SHUT-UP!
PRICE GUIDE
SOX

BUT LOOK AT THIS— I'VE GOT FIRST EDITION PAPERBACKS BY KURT VONNEGUT!
...SURELY SOMEONE IN THIS PLACE DIGS VONNEGUT!
I WOULDN'T COUNT ON IT...
CAT'S CRADLE

SIGH... YOU'RE RIGHT... WHO AM I KIDDING?...
...JUST LOOK AT THE BUSINESS THAT GUY YAHTZI MURPHY'S DOING... HE SELLS NOTHING BUT VIDEOS THESE DAYS...
VIDEOS ARE THE WAY TO GO, SINCE WATCHING T.V. TAKES ZERO EFFORT... EVEN READING COMIC BOOKS TAKES EFFORT...
GRRRRR... YAHTZI MURPHY... I HATE THAT GUY...
YAHTZI'S MONSTERMANIA

OH, REALLY? I CAN'T IMAGINE WHY...
I BOUGHT A COPY OF "THE GIRL CAN'T HELP IT" FROM HIM, WHICH TURNED OUT TO BE A TOTALLY UNWATCHABLE, TENTH GENERATION BOOTLEG...

...AND EVERY TIME I TRY TO TALK TO HIM ABOUT IT HE JUST BLOWS ME OFF...
HE'D RATHER DIE THAN GIVE UP ONE RED CENT...

FORGET ABOUT EVER GETTING YOUR MONEY BACK FROM HIM...ONCE HE GETS HIS MITTS ON YOUR DOUGH HE'LL NEVER LET GO...
SOUNDS LIKE YOU'VE HAD TROUBLE WITH HIM TOO...
YEAH, HE'S BURNED ME A FEW TIMES, THOUGH I CAN'T SAY I HATE HIM FOR IT...
I'VE KNOWN HIM SINCE HE WAS TWELVE...HE USED TO COME INTO MY SHOP, BACK WHEN I HAD A SHOP...

HE CAME FROM A MESSED-UP FAMILY— HALF IRISH AND HALF SIAMESE, IF YOU CAN IMAGINE THAT...
NO ONE COULD PRONOUNCE HIS NAME RIGHT, SO WE ALL CALLED HIM "YAHTZI" INSTEAD...
IT USED TO PISS HIM OFF... BUT NOW HE'S STUCK WITH IT...
HEH HEH...
ASK ME ABOUT THE LIBERTARIAN PARTY
KEMPER/CON
STEVE CHABBA

* SIGH *... I DUNNO... YEAH, THE GUY'S A CROOK, BUT WHO ISN'T THESE DAYS...
EVERYONE'S TRYING TO GET AWAY WITH AS MUCH AS THEY POSSIBLY CAN, AND YOU JUST HAVE TO KEEP THAT IN MIND WHEN YOU'RE DEALING WITH GUYS LIKE HIM...
SOMETIMES YOU'VE GOT TO LOWER YOUR STANDARDS...YOU CAN'T ALWAYS CHOOSE WHO YOU DO BUSINESS WITH...
YEAH, SURE, WHATEVER YOU SAY...

LOOK BUD, JUST FORGET IT, OKAY? MURPHY'S HAD THE SHIT BEATEN OUT OF HIM AT LEAST A DOZEN TIMES ALREADY...
IT'S OBVIOUS HE'S NEVER GONNA LEARN...
YEAH, WELL, YOU NEVER KNOW...MAYBE ONE MORE BEATING MIGHT DO THE TRICK...

OH, I SEE, YOU'RE A TOUGH GUY, HUH? PARDON ME FOR NOT REALIZING IT SOONER...
LOOK MAN, WHY DON'T YOU ADD A NIP OF THIS TO YOUR COFFEE AND MELLOW OUT FOR A WHILE—YOU STILL PARTAKE, DON'T YOU?
I BOUGHT MY T.V. ALONG, AND THE SONICS GAME STARTS IN FIVE MINUTES...
NO THANKS. I'VE GOT TO GO...

SUIT YERSELF, BUT DON'T SAY I DIDN'T WARN YOU...
STUPID KID...
REVENGE
...BUT FIRST, SOME SCORES FROM AROUND THE N.B.A...

A FEW MINUTES LATER...

THINK YOU'RE PRETTY CUTE, HUH, BRADLEY? IS THIS YOUR WAY OF GETTING EVEN?
HEY, YOU OWE ME, MAN, AND YOU KNOW IT!

I DON'T OWE YOU NOTHING!!! I NEVER OWED ANYONE A GODDAMNED THING, YOU GOT THAT?!
HEY, LEAVE HIM ALONE, YOU ASSHOLE!
YIKES!

—HUH? WHO ARE YOU CALLING AN ASSHOLE!?
(LISA! SHHH!)
I'M CALLING YOU AN ASSHOLE, ASSHOLE!

YOU GOT WHAT YOU WANTED MISTER! NOW WHY DON'T YOU GET LOST!
...AND NEXT TIME TRY PICKING ON SOMEONE YOUR OWN SIZE FOR A CHANGE!
I...UH... *GULP!*
ACK! ACK!

ARRGH... ALL RIGHT... I GUESS I MADE MY POINT...
BUT SEE HERE, BRADLEY, THE NEXT TIME YOU'VE GOT A BONE TO PICK WITH ME TRY ACTING LIKE A MAN FOR A CHANGE AND DEAL WITH ME FACE TO FACE!
NONE OF THIS STEALING FROM ME AND THEN HAVING YOUR LADY FRIEND SAVE YOUR ASS — DIG ME?
YEAH, YEAH, YEAH...

WHAT'S THE STORY WITH THAT GUY? WHOEVER HE IS HE OUGHT TO BE SHOT!
IT'S A LONG STORY...
...RIGHT NOW I JUST FEEL LIKE PACKING UP AND GOING HOME...

SO WHAT'S THE FINAL VERDICT, BUDDY? WAS IT A TOTAL LOSS?
NAH. WE FLEECED A COUPLE OF TEENAGERS PRETTY GOOD. OTHER THAN THAT IT WAS ALL NICKEL AND DIME STUFF.
HOW ABOUT YOU?
EXHIBITION HALL SERVICE ENTRANCE
TOYOTA

OH, I WOUND UP DOING ALL RIGHT...
FUCKING SONICS, THOUGH...THEY WERE BEATING UTAH BY 16 POINTS AT THE END OF THE THIRD QUARTER, BUT THEY TOTALLY BLEW IT IN THE FINAL MINUTES...
I GOT SO PISSED I SPILLED MY COFFEE ALL OVER MY PANTS...

SERVES ME RIGHT FOR FORGETTING THAT ALL SEATTLE TEAMS SUCK—THAT THEY ALWAYS SUCKED AND ALWAYS WILL SUCK...
STILL, I CAN'T HELP HOPING...
YOU'RE A HOPELESS IDEALIST, STEVE, THAT'S YOUR PROBLEM...

I GUESS YOU'RE RIGHT...
SO ARE WE ALL PACKED UP AND READY TO GO, THEN?
LOOKS LIKE IT...
HUFF *PUFF*

AND HOW ABOUT YOU, LISA? DID YOU ENJOY YOUR FIRST DAY OF SELF-EMPLOYMENT?
IT WAS ALL RIGHT...I'D BE WILLING TO TRY IT AGAIN...
COMING SOON TO THIS SITE: HUNTINGTON TOWERS 32 UNITS

...IT'S NOT LIKE I'VE GOT ANYTHING BETTER TO DO...
HUH? OH, SURE, GO AHEAD...
...HEY, CAN I TURN THE RADIO ON?

OH, WOW! THE COLLEGE STATION IS ACTUALLY PLAYING A SONG BY ROYAL TRUX!
THE ROYAL WHA?!

ROYAL TRUX! THEY'RE THIS REALLY COOL JUNKIE BAND FROM NEW YORK CITY!
OH YEAH, RIGHT. NOW WOULD YOU MIND CHANGING THE STATION?

WHAT? NO WAY! THESE GUYS ARE GREAT!
DON'T TRY TO BULLSHIT ME. THIS STUFF IS UTTER GARBAGE. NO ONE IN THEIR RIGHT MIND WOULD DIG THIS NONSENSE.

HEY MAN, I KNOW A LOT OF PEOPLE WHO DIG THIS STUFF!
THEN A LOT OF PEOPLE ARE BRAIN-WASHED... "GRUNGE ROCK"— WHAT A HOAX!
I'M WITH YOU, STEVE—THIS SO-CALLED "MUSIC" IS BEYOND THE PALE ...

BOY OH BOY, LISTEN TO YOU TWO! YOU GUYS HATE EVERYTHING, DON'T YOU?
YOU'RE JUST LIKE TWO PEAS IN A POD!
SORRY TO OFFEND, MISSY.
JUST TELLIN' IT LIKE IT IS...

LATER, AT BUDDY'S PAD...
(PSST, HEY BUD! LISA'S LOOKIN' PRETTY HOT IN THAT GET-UP OF HERS...)
YA THINK SO, HUH?

UM-HMMM! SAY, DO ME A FAVOR AND GIVE HER AN EXTRA SHTUPPIN' TONIGHT, JUST FOR ME, WILL YA?
HEY! WATCH WHAT YOU SAY!

CALM DOWN, BOY! I WAS JUST FUNNIN' WITH YA...
DON'T BE SO TOUCHY...
HEH! HEH!
OH, WELL...OKAY THEN...
SMEK! SMEK!

ARRRGH... DISGUSTING OLD GEEZER...
I DREAD THE THOUGHT OF SOMEDAY WINDING UP JUST LIKE HIM, EVEN THOUGH I PROBABLY WILL...
LISA'S RIGHT—WE ARE TWO PEAS IN A POD!
HEH-HEH...

AND SO...
WELP, I GUESS THAT TAKES CARE OF MY STUFF...
NOT QUITE...

...YOU FORGOT THIS BAG FULL OF VIDEOS...
?!? BUT, THAT'S NOT MINE...
FOOD GIANT

I'LL TAKE THAT...
SNATCH!
HUH?
?!?
ZIP!

I'LL SEE YOU LATER, BUDDY!
WHA? OH, SEE YA! AND THANKS FOR THE LIFT...
OH LISA, CAN I TALK TO YOU FOR A SECOND—
NO!

WHADDAYA MEAN, NO?!? I JUST WANNA KNOW WHERE ALL THOSE VIDEOS CAME FROM...
ONLY IF YOU PROMISE NOT TO GET MAD AT ME, 'CUZ I DID IT FOR YOU!

DID WHAT FOR ME?! I DON'T GET IT...
WELL, I WAS SO PISSED OFF AT THAT YAHTZI CHARACTER FOR GIVING YOU A HARD TIME THAT WHILE YOU WERE BUSY PACKING UP OUR STUFF I SNUCK UP BEHIND HIS BOOTH AND STOLE THE FIRST THING I COULD LAY MY HANDS ON...

YOU WHAT?!? YOU MEAN THIS STUFF BELONGS TO YAHTZI?
HOLY SHIT, LISA! DO YOU REALIZE WHAT YOU'VE DONE?!
SO I STOLE SOMETHING, SO WHAT? SINCE WHEN ARE YOU ABOVE STEALING STUFF?
BESIDES, HE DESERVED IT!

THAT'S TOTALLY BESIDES THE POINT! YOU SAW WITH YOUR OWN EYES WHAT A MADMAN HE IS!
ONCE HE FIGURES OUT WHAT HAPPENED I'M A DEAD MAN!
BUT HE WON'T FIGURE IT OUT! HOW COULD HE? NO ONE SAW ME TAKE IT, AND YOU WERE OUTSIDE AT THE TIME, SO—

BUT NONE OF THAT MATTERS! HE'LL JUST ASSUME I DID IT AND THEN COME OVER HERE LOOKING FOR IT, WHERE HE WILL FIND IT AND THEN I'LL BE HISTORY!!!
JESUS, BUDDY... CALM DOWN...

YOU'RE GETTING AWFULLY CARRIED AWAY... DON'T BE SO PARANOID...
NOTHING'S GOING TO HAPPEN...
B-B-BUT HOW CAN YOU BE SO SURE...

TSK JUST TRUST ME, OKAY? I'M A GOOD STEALER!
NOW LET'S OPEN A FEW BEERS AND CELEBRATE OUR FIRST DAY AS PRIVATE ENTREPRENEURS...
YEAH, YOU'RE RIGHT... THIS SHOULD BE A DAY OF CELEBRATION...

THAT'S RIGHT! SO LET'S MAKE A TOAST — TO US!
NOW LET'S KICK BACK, RELAX, AND ENJOY SOME OF OUR NEW MOVIES!
OKAY, SOUNDS LIKE A PLAN... HEH-HEH...
CLINK!

LATER THAT EVENING...
...THAT "CARNIVAL OF SOULS" WAS PRETTY COOL...
...IT WAS VERY DREAM-LIKE...
I WISH MY DREAMS WERE THAT COOL!
LET'S WATCH "SPIDER BABY" NEXT, OKAY?
THE END

BANG! BANG! BANG!
GULP! D-DID YOU HEAR A NOISE?
Y-YOU MEAN LIKE SOMEONE POUNDING ON OUR DOOR? I DON'T TH-THINK SO...

OPEN UP, BUDDY! I KNOW YOU'RE IN THERE!

OMIGOD! IT'S YAHTZI MURPHY! WHAT'LL WE DO?!
LET'S PRETEND WE'RE NOT HOME AND MAYBE HE'LL GO AWAY...

IT'S NO USE PRETENDING YOU'RE NOT HOME, BRADLEY! OPEN UP OR I'LL BREAK YOUR DOOR DOWN!!!
OMIGOD! OMIGOD! OMIGOD!
QUICK, HIDE ALL THE MOVIES!
WHERE'D THAT SHOPPING BAG GO?! THESE TAPES ARE SCATTERED ALL OVER THE PLACE! OMIGOD, OMIGOD...
AAH, FUCK THIS SHIT, MAN!
I'M GONNA PUT AN END TO THIS NONSENSE ONCE AND FOR ALL!

(LISA, NO! DON'T OPEN THAT DOOR!)
DON'T WORRY ABOUT ME! I KNOW HOW TO DEAL WITH THE LIKES OF HIM!

OPEN UP, MAN, BEFORE I START TO LOSE MY COOL!
KEEP YOUR SHIRT ON, ASS-HOLE!
...HAIL MARY, FULL OF GRACE...

WHAT DO YOU WANT? WHAT-EVER IT IS WE GAVE AT THE OFFICE...
WELL, WELL, IF IT ISN'T THE LITTLE WOMAN, COVERING BUDDY'S ASS FOR HIM AGAIN, EH?
OPEN THE DOOR, SWEETHEART. I CAME TO RETRIEVE SOMETHING OF MINE...

I KNOW IT WAS *YOU* WHO STOLE 'EM, SINCE NOONE ELSE WOULD BE STUPID ENOUGH TO PULL SUCH AN OBVIOUS STUNT!!!

GRRRRR... YOU REALLY DID IT THIS TIME, BUDDY... YOU JUST DUG YOUR OWN GRAVE...
OH YEAH? SO WHAT ARE YOU GONNA DO ABOUT IT, PAL? TAKE ONE STEP CLOSER AND I'LL DO TO YOUR SKULL WHAT I DID TO YOUR LOUSY MOVIES...
KILL HIM, BUDDY! KIL'L HIM!

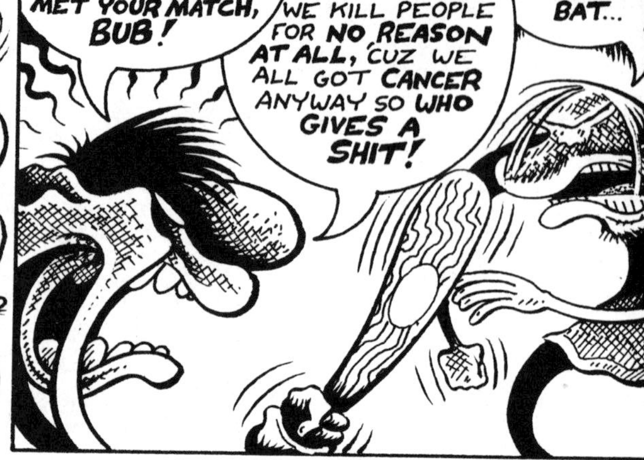

YOU ALWAYS GOT AWAY WITH MURDER 'CUZ PEOPLE WERE AFRAID OF YOUR PSYCHO ROUTINE, BUT YOU JUST MET YOUR MATCH, BUB!
I'M FROM NEW JERSEY, MAN! IN JERSEY WE KILL PEOPLE FOR NO REASON AT ALL, 'CUZ WE ALL GOT CANCER ANYWAY SO WHO GIVES A SHIT!
YEAH, YEAH, YOU'RE ALL TALK!
NOW GIMME THAT BAT...

YOU WANT IT? HERE!
SWOOSH!
WHOA!
YEAH! GET 'IM!

JEEZUS! YOU REALLY ARE CRAZY!
ALL RIGHT, I'M OUTTA HERE, BUT YOU'RE STILL GONNA PAY FOR THIS, BRADLEY...
WHATEVER YOU DISH OUT I'LL PAY YOU BACK IN SPADES, MAN...

YEAH, RIGHT... WE'LL SEE ABOUT THAT, BUT YOU MIGHT AS WELL FORGET ABOUT ANY PLANS YOU HAVE OF GOING INTO THE COLLECTOR BUSINESS IN THIS TOWN, 'CUZ I'VE GOT CONNECTIONS, MAN, AND I'LL SEE TO IT THAT YOU'LL NEVER BE ABLE TO—
BLOW IT OUT YOUR HOLE!

YEAH, GET OUT BEFORE I STAB YOU WITH MY KNIFE!
GOOD LORD! YOU'RE BOTH NUTS!

...NICE CHATTING WITH YOU, BUDDY, AND I HOPE YOU LIKE YOUR CURRENT JOB, 'CUZ YOU'RE GONNA BE THERE A LONG TIME...
I SAID GET OUT!
YIKES!

SLAM!
ZING—P-TWANG!
OH MY GOD!

YES! WHOO-HOO! WE SHOWED HIM A THING OR TWO, DIDN'T WE, BUDDY!

...BUDDY? ARE YOU OKAY?
I-I-I-I-T...
OH MY GOD, WHAT HAVE I DONE?!

OH, C'MON, BUDDY! YOU SHOULD BE PROUD OF YOURSELF! WE GAVE THAT PSYCHO-PATH A TASTE OF HIS OWN MEDICINE!
"PSYCHO-PATH"...YEAH, RIGHT... LIKE WE SHOULD TALK...

YOU CAME AWFULLY CLOSE TO HIT-TING HIM WITH THAT KNIFE, LISA...
CLOSE? I WANTED TO HIT HIM! I WANTED TO DRIVE THAT KNIFE RIGHT THROUGH HIS SKULL!

BUT...WHY? WHY WOULD YOU TRY TO KILL HIM WHEN HE WAS AL-READY OUT THE DOOR?
BECAUSE HE WAS MEAN TO YOU, BUDDY! I'D KILL ANY-ONE WHO GIVES YOU A HARD TIME, AND I MEAN IT!

OH MY GOD...
WHAT!? WHAT I'D SAY?!

...OH, I GET IT! YOU THINK THIS IS ALL MY FAULT, DON'T YOU!?
YOU PROBABLY THINK I'M NOTHING BUT TROUBLE, HUH?
NO I DON'T...
TRUDGE... TRUDGE...

YES YOU DO, AND YOU'RE PROBABLY RIGHT!
I TRY TO HELP, BUT ALL I DO IS MESS EVERYTHING UP!
YOU MUST HATE ME!
OH NO I DON'T... C'MERE...
BOO-HOO-HOO!

YES YOU DO! YOU HATE EVERYTHING ELSE, SO WHY WOULDN'T YOU HATE ME AS WELL?
NOW, NOW, I DON'T HATE YOU... YOU'RE PROBABLY THE ONLY PERSON I DON'T HATE...
SOB!

R-R-R- REALLY?
UH-HUH, AND I'M TOUCHED THAT YOU'D BE SO WILLING TO KILL FOR ME FOR THE SLIGHTEST OF PRETEXTS...
IT MAKES ME QUESTION YOUR SANITY, BUT I'M TOUCHED NONETHELESS...

SNIFF THAT'S NICE OF YOU TO SAY, BUDDY, BUT STILL, I SHOULD'VE NEVER STOLEN THOSE VIDEOS... IT WAS STUPID OF ME... NOT TO MENTION WRONG...
OH NO IT WASN'T... YOU HAD EVERY RIGHT TO STEAL FROM HIM... IT WAS A MORALLY JUSTIFIABLE ACT...
JESUS WOULD APPROVE...

SNIFF ...YA THINK SO?
I KNOW SO!
TOO BAD WE GOT CAUGHT, THOUGH...
HONK!

YEAH, TOO BAD...
I REALLY WANTED TO SEE "SPIDER BABY"...

AND NOW IT LOOKS LIKE OUR CAREERS AS "DEALERS IN KOOL KOLLECTABLES" HAS BEEN NIPPED IN THE BUD...
YEAH, BUT WHO KNOWS... MAYBE IT WAS A BLESSING IN DISGUISE, SINCE I'M NOT TOO SURE WE'RE CUT OUT FOR THIS RACKET...
NOTHING'S MORE PATHETIC —OR DANGEROUS— THAN BEING A SECOND-RATE HUSTLER...

MMM YEAH, I SUPPOSE, THOUGH I KINDA LIKE THE SOUND OF THAT: "SECOND-RATE HUSTLER"
IT'S GOT A NICE RING TO IT...
YEAH, YOU WOULD...

..HEY, LOOK! HERE'S A MOVIE THAT SURVIVED THE CARNAGE IN TACT...
OH YEAH? WHICH ONE IS IT?

"THE TINGLER"...
IT'S GOT VINCENT PRICE IN IT...
YA WANNA WATCH IT?
OH, OKAY...

...ALTHOUGH I WAS KIND OF THINKING THAT WE COULD HAVE SEX INSTEAD...
SEX? ...NOW?

SURE! WHY NOT? DON'T YOU WANNA?
WELL... OKAY...ONLY I'D LIKE TO WATCH THIS MOVIE AS WELL...

SO WE'LL DO BOTH AT THE SAME TIME! I'VE GOT NO OBJECTIONS TO THAT...
ALL RIGHT THEN, I'LL GO POP THE TAPE IN...

CLICK! WHRRRR...

..Y'KNOW WHAT, BUDDY? I GOT REALLY TURNED ON WHEN YOU TOOK A SWING AT YAHTZI'S HEAD WITH THAT BASEBALL BAT...
OH YEAH?
SHLORP!

UM-HMM! MY PUSSY STARTED JUICIN' LIKE CRAZY!
HUH. WELL, I GUESS I'LL HAVE TO ASSAULT MY ENEMIES MORE OFTEN, IF THAT'S WHAT M'LADY DESIRES...
F.B.I. WARNING

COULD YOU? I'D APPRECIATE IT...
...AND REMEMBER, A SCREAM IN TIME MAY SAVE YOUR LIFE!

THE END

STINKY BROWN, SUPER STAR

FEATURING FLAIR MEENER, STAR-MAKER!

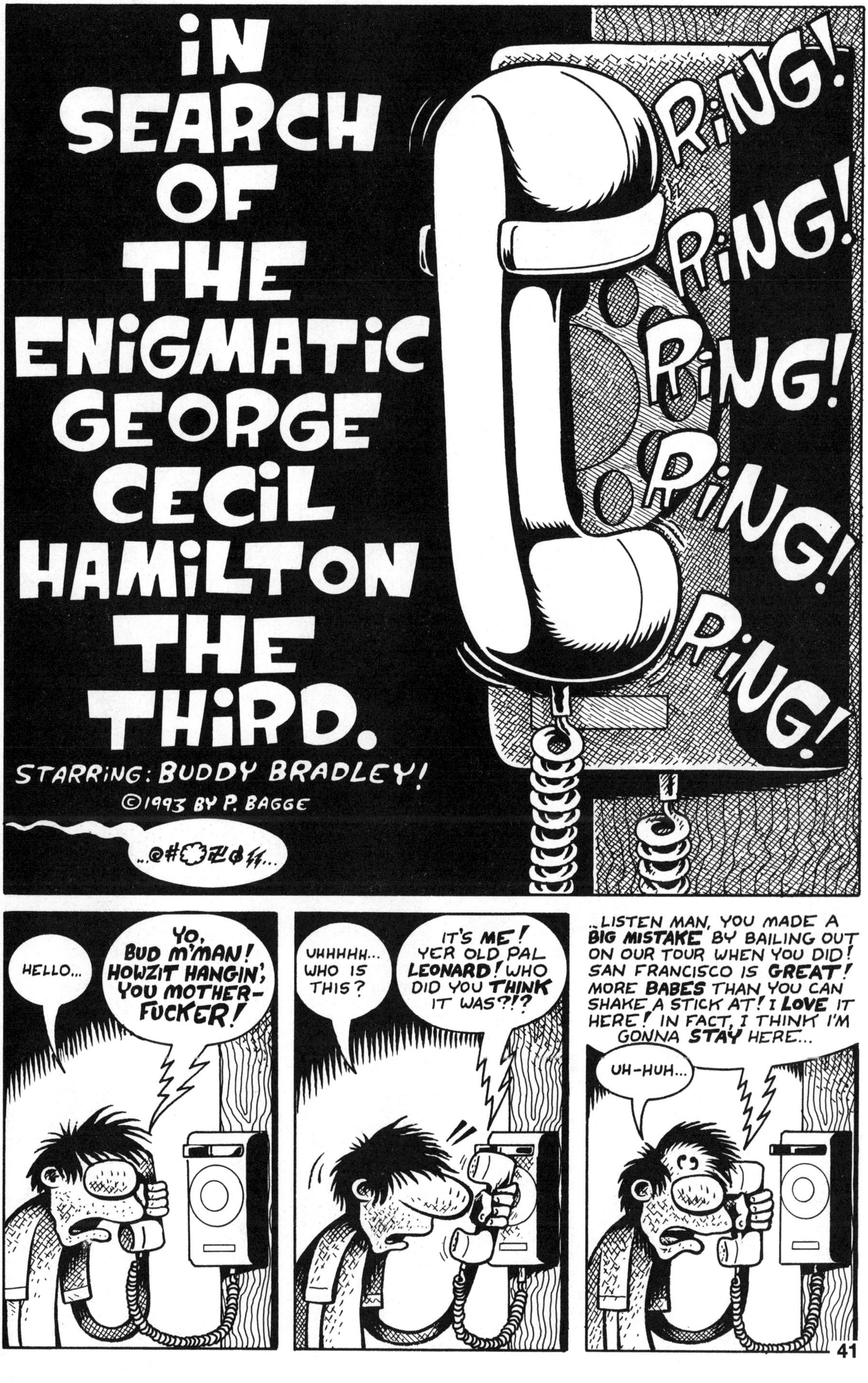

IN SEARCH OF THE ENIGMATIC GEORGE CECIL HAMILTON THE THIRD.

STARRING: BUDDY BRADLEY!

©1993 BY P. BAGGE

SO, LIKE, UH, WHATEVER HAPPENED TO THE OTHER BAND MEMBERS, LIKE WHATZISNAME, UMM...
WHO KNOWS AND WHO CARES!!! I'VE HAD IT WITH THOSE FUCKS! WHO NEEDS 'EM!?

UH-HUH... SO, WHAT HAVE YOU BEEN DOING...
OH, I'M GETTING BY, ONE WAY OR ANOTHER—WHICH REMINDS ME OF THE MAIN REASON I'M CALLING YOU...

UH-OH, HERE IT COMES...
NOW DON'T PANIC! I'M NOT GONNA HIT YOU UP FOR ANY MONEY! ALL I'M ASKING IS FOR YOU TO CHECK MY ROOM FOR ANYTHING VALUABLE...

"VALUABLE"? LIKE WHAT?
OH, YOU KNOW! LIKE OLD RECORDS, OR, I DUNNO... DRUGS OR SOMETHING...

AND THEN WHAT AM I SUPPOSED TO DO, SELL THEM FOR YOU? NO WAY—
,THEN SEND 'EM TO ME AND I'LL SELL THEM! JUST DO IT NOW 'CAUSE I'M DESPERATE!! PULLEEZE—

OKAY, OKAY, I'LL LOOK AND SEE WHAT I CAN DIG UP...
THANKS, MAN! ...OH, BY THE WAY, DID YOU SEE THE LATEST ISSUE OF ZYGOTE?

"ZYGOTE"? YOU MEAN GEORGE'S LIL XEROXED MAGAZINE? WHY WOULD I BE READING THAT THING?
OH MAN, YOU GOTTA CHECK IT OUT! THERE'S A BIG ARTICLE ON YOU IN THERE! AND IT AIN'T NICE, LEMME TELL YA...

AN ARTICLE ON ME? BUT... WHY?
WELL, IT ISN'T JUST ABOUT YOU, HE JUST USES YOU AS AN EXAMPLE OF WHAT'S WRONG WITH THE YOUTH OF TODAY, OR SOME SUCH NONSENSE...
OH MAN, YA GOTTA CHECK IT OUT! YOU'RE GONNA SHIT!

BUT I DON'T EVEN KNOW WHERE GEORGE LIVES, SO — HEY, HOW DID YOU GET A HOLD OF A COPY?
I FOUND IT IN A HEALTH FOOD STORE ON HAIGHT ST... THEY HAD A GREAT BIG PILE OF 'EM!

ON HAIGHT ST.? HOW CAN THAT BE? I THOUGHT HE ONLY MADE ENOUGH COPIES TO SEND TO ALL OF HIS "PEERS."
THIS MUST BE SOME KIND OF FLUKE...
MAYBE. WHO KNOWS? BUT IF YOU CAN'T FIND A COPY I'LL SEND YOU MINE, 'CUZ YOU GOTTA SEE THIS THING!

WELL, NOW, WHAT EXACTLY DOES IT SAY ABOUT ME? DO YOU HAVE IT IN FRONT OF YOU?
WELL, I'M NOT GONNA READ IT OVER THE PHONE, 'CUZ THE ARTICLE'S WAY TOO LONG...

...ALL I'LL SAY IS THAT IF YOU EVER DECIDE TO SUE FOR LIBEL I OUGHT TO GET 10% FOR BRINGING IT TO YOUR ATTENTION.... HEH-HEH...
JEEZ, IS IT THAT BAD?

LOOK MAN, I'VE SAID ENOUGH. JUST SEND ME MY MONEY AND I'LL SEND YOU THE ARTICLE, OKAY? THANKS!
WAIT! I—

CLICK!
HUH.

...I WONDER WHAT THIS "ZYGOTE" BUSINESS IS REALLY ALL ABOUT...
WHY WOULD GEORGE WANT TO ATTACK ME IN PRINT? I NEVER DID ANYTHING TO HIM!

AAH, STINKY MUST'VE BEEN PUTTING ME ON, OR AT LEAST EXAGGERATING TO SOME DEGREE, JUST TO GET A REACTION OUTTA ME...

BESIDES, I'VE GOT MORE IMPORTANT THINGS TO WORRY ABOUT THAN SOME CRUDDY LITTLE FANZINE THAT NOBODY READS...
PLOP!

...LIKE FOR EXAMPLE HOW I'M GONNA PAY STINKY BACK FOR ALL THOSE RECORDS OF HIS I ALREADY SOLD...

THE NEXT DAY...
2HR PARKING 9-6
ELLOPHANE
...I HOPE I CAN GET SOMETHING FOR WHAT'S LEFT OF STINKY'S RECORD COLLECTION...

TAKE ONE
Stranger

WHILE I'M HERE I MIGHT AS WELL GRAB A COPY OF SOME OF THESE FREEBIE PUBLICATIONS...

?!?
WHAT'S THIS?! THIS COULDN'T BE GEORGE'S 'ZINE, COULD IT?
TWENTY-THREE
ZYGOTE
TAKE ONE
WORDS FROM THE HIGH-TECH WO...
...PUTER NETWORKS AS UMBILICAL COR...
THE DEATH OF "CYBERPUNK"
SLACKING SLACKERS

OH MY GOD, IT IS! AND LOOK AT HOW SLICK IT IS ALL OF A SUDDEN! COLOR COVERS AND EVERYTHING!
HOW ON EARTH DID HE GET UP THE MONEY TO...
ZYGOTE

—AND IT'S FOR FREE?! WHY, THIS IS INSANE!
THIS MEANS THAT EVERYONE IN TOWN WILL BE PICKING UP A COPY OF THIS!

LET'S SEE, WHERE'S THAT FRIGGIN' ARTICLE STINKY WAS TALKING ABOUT...
I GUESS THIS MUST BE IT...
IS THERE ANY H...
...ENERATIO...
X?
...ALL TO ARMS BY ...DITORS OF ZYGOTE

HMMM...THIS ISN'T ABOUT ME! IT'S JUST YER TYPICAL "TWENTY-SOMETHING" BULLSHIT, ABOUT HOW WE GOTTA GET OUR SHIT TOGETHER AND BLAH, BLAH, BLAH...
I DON'T SEE MY NAME ANY—
WAIT A MINUTE! WHAT'S THIS?
ZYGOTE

..."A CASE IN POINT WOULD BE SOMEONE I HAD THE MISFORTUNE TO SHARE AN APARTMENT WITH A WHILE BACK WHO WENT BY THE NAME OF 'BUDDY'—SOME OF YOU MAY EVEN KNOW HIM, BUT EVEN IF YOU DON'T I'M SURE YOU'RE FAMILIAR WITH HIS TYPE"...

FIVE MINUTES LATER...
..."THAT THERE ARE SO MANY OF THESE 'BUDDIES' AMONG US REPRESENTS NOT ONLY A FAILURE OF OUR MASS CULTURE AND EDUCATIONAL SYSTEM, BUT A FAILURE BY THE MORE ENLIGHTENED AMONG US FOR EVEN TOLERATING THE LIKES OF THEM, WITH THEIR NEGATIVE ATTITUDES AND REACTIONARY OPINIONS"...
..."IF WE ARE TO HAVE A CONSTRUCTIVE FUTURE WE MUST FIRST PURGE THESE CANCEROUS BEINGS FROM OUR OWN RANKS BEFORE THEY POISON US ALL"...

RUMPLE! CRUMPLE!

HOW DARE HE! HOW FUCKIN' DARE HE! JUST WHO IN THE HELL DOES HE THINK HE IS?!?
I OUGHTA TRACK HIM DOWN AND...AND KILL HIM!
CAN I HELP YOU? YOU'VE BEEN STANDING THERE FOR A LONG TIME...

...BUT FIRST I'D BETTER CONFISCATE ALL THE OTHER COPIES BEFORE ANYONE ELSE READS THIS...
UH, EXCUSE ME, BUT I DON'T THINK YOU SHOULD BE TAKING ALL OF THOSE...
SCOOP! SCOOP! SCOOP!

...I'D BETTER HURRY AND CHECK ALL THE OTHER LIKELY LOCATIONS FOR COPIES TOO, OR MY NAME'LL BE MUD!
HEY!!!!

HOURS LATER...

HMMMM... MAYBE I SHOULD CHECK OUT THIS PLACE, TOO...

HEY, BUDDY! LOOKING FOR SOMEONE?
HEAD EAST

HUH? OH, HI....
ACTUALLY, I'M LOOKING TO SEE IF THEY HAVE ANY COPIES OF A MAGAZINE CALLED "ZYGOTE"...
OH, YOU MEAN THIS THING?
ZYGOTE

WHERE DID YOU GET THAT?!?
THEY HAD A HUGE PILE OF 'EM BY THE DOOR YESTERDAY...
THIS IS THE LAST ONE, I'M AFRAID...
ZOOM!

SIGH TOO LATE, JUST AS I FEARED...
WELL HERE, HAVE MY COPY IF YOU WANT IT THAT BAD...
HEY, DID YOU KNOW YOU'RE MENTIONED IN IT, BUDDY?

OF COURSE I KNOW! THAT'S WHY I'M TRYING TO CONFISCATE AS MANY COPIES AS I CAN! CAN YOU BELIEVE ALL THE LIES THEY WROTE ABOUT ME?!?
LIES?! WHAT LIES?! WHERE?
TO TELL YOU THE TRUTH I JUST GLANCED THROUGH IT AND HAPPENED TO CATCH YOUR NAME...
WHY, IS IT REALLY THAT BAD?
IT'S BAD, IT'S BAD... READ IT FOR YOURSELVES, IF YOU MUST...
...OH MY... I DIDN'T KNOW YOU WERE A REGISTERED REPUBLICAN...
AND YOU STOLE FROM YOUR OWN MOTHER? *TSK, TSK*...
ZYGOTE
ZYGOTE

I ONLY TOOK A FEW BUCKS FROM HER PURSE! WHO DIDN'T PULL SHIT LIKE THAT WHEN THEY WERE A KID?!
PLUS I'M PROUD TO SAY I'VE NEVER VOTED ONCE IN MY WHOLE LIFE!
YEAH, WELL, I WOULDN'T WORRY TOO MUCH ABOUT IT. NOBODY TAKES THESE LITTLE "RANTZINES" SERIOUSLY ANYWAY...
...LISTENS TO RUSH LIMBAUGH... ...JEEZUS...

...I THINK IT WAS NIETZSCHE WHO ONCE SAID:"I DON'T CARE WHAT THEY WRITE ABOUT ME AS LONG AS THEY SPELL MY NAME RIGHT"...
...OR SOMETHING TO THAT EFFECT...
YEAH, I SUPPOSE YOU'RE RIGHT...
OH, BUDDY...

...IS IT TRUE THAT YOU HATE THE JEWS?
?!? THAT I WHAT?!?
OH—HEH! HEH!—WELL, IF YOU'RE REFERRING TO SOMETHING YOU READ IN THERE, I CAN EXPLAIN...
ZYGOTE

..(WELL, JUST BETWEEN YOU AND ME, I FEEL THE SAME WAY)...
WHUH? YOU DO? BUT I—

(UH-HUH! THE WAY THEY OWN AND CONTROL EVERYTHING? IT'S DISGUSTING!)
...('CEPT YOU, THAT IS)...
(BACK WHERE I CAME FROM EVERYONE KNEW IT AND WASN'T AFRAID TO SAY IT, BUT UP HERE PEOPLE ARE... BRAINWASHED OR SOMETHING)...
BUT, I NEVER—
A JEW

HERE'S MY NUMBER, IN CASE YOU DON'T HAVE IT ALREADY...
CALL ME IF YOU'RE NOT BUSY THIS WEEKEND!
...BUT...

WELL, WELL! IT LOOKS LIKE ANTI-SEMITIC LOVE IS IN THE AIR...
B-B-BUT I...

DON'T FIGHT IT, BUDDY! IT'S BIGGER THAN THE BOTH OF YOU!
OH SHUT UP...
JUST WAIT 'TIL I REPORT HER TO THE ELDERS OF ZION! SHE'LL BE OUT OF A JOB WITHIN TWO WEEKS!

LATER THAT EVENING...

...AND THEN HE SAYS I HAVE THE "ETHICS OF A REPTILE" JUST BECAUSE I USED SOME OF HIS COUGH MEDICINE WITHOUT HIS PERMISSION AND THEN LEFT THE CAP OFF!
CAN YOU BELIEVE THE NERVE OF THIS GUY?!
Y'KNOW BUDDY, I THINK YOU'RE MAKING WAY TOO BIG A DEAL OUT OF THIS...
PACE!
STOMP!

...BUT WHAT GETS ME THE MOST IS HOW HE'LL TAKE OFF ON THIS NEW MALCOLM X ROUTINE WHENEVER IT SUITS HIS PURPOSES...
THERE'S ALL THIS TALK ABOUT A CONSPIRACY TO SUPPRESS "AFRICAN-AMERICAN CULTURE", AND THAT I'M SOMEHOW A PART OF IT!
YEAH, WELL, THAT'S HIS PREROGATIVE, AFTER ALL...
STAY TUNED FOR "FULL HOUSE."

BUT WHAT DOES HE KNOW ABOUT IT, OR EVEN CARE, THAT OREO COOKIE! HE'S THE WHITEST ACTING GUY I KNOW!
HE'S JUST USING THE COLOR OF HIS SKIN TO STACK THE DECK AGAINST ME, THAT NO GOOD S.O.B...
BUDDY, SERIOUSLY, I THINK YOU'RE...

... AND IF HE MUST DISCUSS MY PERSONAL LIFE HE OUGHT TO AT LEAST GET HIS FACTS STRAIGHT! LIKE THIS PART, WHERE HE CLAIMS I WAS SCREWING MY "LONG SUFFERING GIRLFRIEND"'S ROOMMATE BEHIND HER BACK...
HE SAID WHAT?!?
GRAB!
LET ME SEE THAT THING!
?!? BUT, I THOUGHT YOU WEREN'T INTERESTED...
..."HER SLEAZY ROOMMATE"? IS THAT SUPPOSED TO BE ME? IS HE TALKING ABOUT ME?!?
WHO ELSE WOULD HE BE REFERRING TO?

BUT, THIS IS A TOTAL LIE! WHAT IS HE TRYING TO DO TO ME? HOW DARE HE TRY TO INSINUATE THAT I... THAT I...
ZYGOTE

ISN'T THERE A LAW AGAINST THIS?!?
NOW YOU KNOW HOW I FEEL.
ZYGOTE

WHERE DOES THIS GUY LIVE? I FEEL LIKE TRACKING HIM DOWN AND...AND KILLING HIM!!!
I WISH I KNEW... I TRIED HIS MOM'S HOUSE AND EVEN SHE DOESN'T KNOW HOW TO REACH HIM...

AND WHERE'D HE GET THE MONEY TO PUT OUT A MAGAZINE LIKE THIS? DOES HE ACTUALLY HAVE FINANCIAL BACKING? WHO ON EARTH WOULD... I MEAN, HOW... WHY WOULD...

...I'M STARTING TO GET PARANOID...
YOU AND ME BOTH, SISTER...

...Y'KNOW, THERE'S ONLY ONE WAY I CAN THINK OF TO GET EVEN WITH HIM...
YOU MEAN...?

THAT'S RIGHT! PUT OUT A FANZINE OF MY OWN!
I'VE TALKED ABOUT IT LONG ENOUGH! THE TIME HAS COME TO ACT!
NOW I HAVE A CAUSE: VENGEANCE!
OH BOY! AND I'LL HELP!

THE FIRST ORDER OF BUSINESS IS FOR ME TO WRITE A COUNTER-ATTACK TO THIS THING! THAT OUGHTA GET THE BALL ROLLING-...THE REST WILL SIMPLY FALL INTO PLACE...
DO YOU KNOW HOW TO TYPE? 'CUZ I SURE DON'T...

WE'LL WORRY ABOUT THE PETTY DETAILS LATER! IN THE MEANTIME I'VE GOT ME A NO-HOLDS-BARRED VINDICTIVE DIATRIBE TO COMPOSE!
GO GET 'EM, BUD! AND I'M GONNA GO OUT AND, UH, ...BUY A STAPLER!

TWO WEEKS LATER...
SO BUDDY, HAVE YOU COME UP WITH ANY IDEAS FOR OUR FANZINE?
OUR WHAT? OH... THAT...
...COMING UP NEXT: MELROSE PLACE!

...NAH... ONCE I WROTE MY REBUTTAL TO GEORGE'S THING I PRETTY MUCH DREW A BLANK...
...I WROTE SOME REVIEWS OF RECORDS AND MOVIES AND STUFF, BUT THEY WERE ALL 100% NEGATIVE, WHICH SORTA CONFIRMED ONE OF GEORGE'S CHARGES AGAINST ME...
SO I THREW 'EM OUT IN ORDER TO MAINTAIN MY OWN CREDIBILITY...

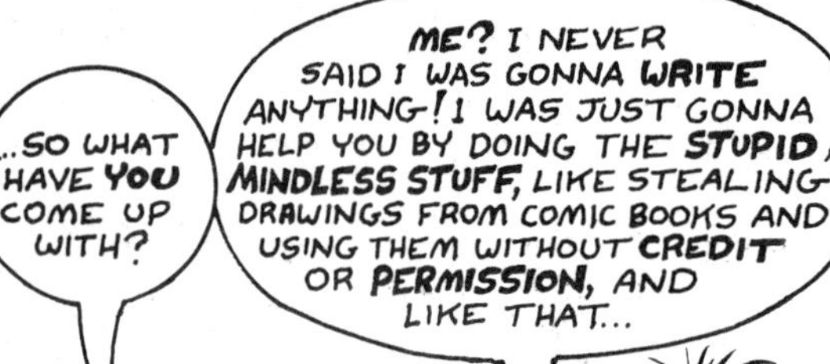

...SO WHAT HAVE YOU COME UP WITH?
ME? I NEVER SAID I WAS GONNA WRITE ANYTHING!! I WAS JUST GONNA HELP YOU BY DOING THE STUPID, MINDLESS STUFF, LIKE STEALING DRAWINGS FROM COMIC BOOKS AND USING THEM WITHOUT CREDIT OR PERMISSION, AND LIKE THAT...

AAH, I DON'T EVEN CARE ANYMORE... I THOUGHT I WAS GONNA CATCH A LOT OF FLAK OVER WHAT GEORGE WROTE ABOUT ME, BUT NO ONE HAS EVEN MENTIONED IT TO ME YET...
I GUESS I OUGHT TO BE RELIEVED, BUT I'M ACTUALLY DISAPPOINTED THAT NOBODY'S SAID A WORD ABOUT THIS...
MY FRIENDS HAVE ALL LET ME DOWN, THANKS TO THEIR GODDAMNED APATHY.

Y'KNOW, I READ SOMEWHERE RECENTLY THAT THIS LACK OF ANY KIND OF MORAL OUTRAGE IS WHAT'S DESTROYING OUR COUNTRY...
WHOEVER WROTE THAT WAS TOTALLY RIGHT ON!
YOU READ THAT IN GEORGE'S ARTICLE ABOUT US...

I DID? OOPS...
...NEVER MIND...
* SIGH *

...WELL NEEDLESS TO SAY OUR "FANZINE" IDEA IS DEAD IN THE WATER, BUT I STILL HAVEN'T GIVEN UP ON MY QUEST FOR VENGEANCE AGAINST GEORGE CECIL HAMILTON THE THIRD...
SO WHAT ARE YOU GONNA DO, LIE ON THE COUCH 'TIL HE BEGS FOR MERCY?

NOT QUITE...I'VE ALREADY CALLED EVERYONE I KNOW WHO KNOWS HIM AND OFFERED A 20 DOLLAR REWARD TO THE FIRST PERSON WHO CAN LEAD ME TO HIS WHEREABOUTS...
"MORAL OUTRAGE"...I'LL SHOW HIM SOME MORAL OUTRAGE...
RING! RING! RING!

I'LL GET IT! THIS COULD BE A LEAD...
DON'T GET YOUR HOPES UP, BUD...
LEAP!
RING! RING!

HELLO? OH, HIYA, ROY! I WAS JUST—
—YOU'RE KIDDING! WHERE? WHEN?

..YOU FOLLOWED HIM TO HIS HOME? GREAT! DID YOU GET THE ADDRESS? ...GREAT! LET'S HAVE IT...
...6TH AVE. WEST...WHERE IS THAT, ON QUEEN ANNE HILL? ..WHAT'S HE DOIN' OVER THERE? ...OH WELL, WHO CARES...
MUNCH!

...HUH? YOU BET I AM! IN FACT I'M GONNA HEAD OVER THERE RIGHT NOW!
...DON'T WORRY, I'LL FILL YOU IN ON EVERYTHING LATER...I'LL EVEN INCLUDE THE AUTOPSY REPORT! YUCK! YUCK!
THANKS FOR THE TIP, MAN! I OWE YA 20!
OH BROTHER...

ISN'T IT KINDA LATE TO BE HEADING OUT?
PERHAPS, BUT I CAN'T AFFORD TO LET THE TRAIL GROW COLD...
DORITOS

WELL, IF YOU DO RUN INTO GEORGE TELL HIM I SAID HI...
WILL DO! BYE!

SLAM!
"AUTOPSY REPORT"...WHO DOES HE THINK HE'S KIDDING...

WOW! WHAT A NICE HOUSE!
I WONDER WHOSE IT IS, AND WHAT GEORGE WOULD BE DOING HERE...
UH-OH, A CAR'S PULLING UP...

HMMM... WHO'S SHE? SHE AIN'T HALF BAD, FOR AN OLDER BROAD...
THIS WHOLE SET-UP DOES NOT ADD UP AT ALL...

OH WELL, I'LL NEVER FIND OUT ANYTHING BY JUST STANDING HERE...

S'CUSE ME, MA'AM, I —
GASP! MY GOODNESS, Y-YOU SCARED ME! W-WHAT DO YOU WANT?

OH—GULP!—WELL, YOU SEE, I'M AN OLD FRIEND OF SOME-ONE NAMED GEORGE HAMILTON, AND I WAS...
A FRIEND OF GEORGE'S? WHY, HOW WONDERFUL! MY NAME IS WINIFRED...
AND YOU ARE?...

OH, MY NAME IS BUDDY... I DO HAVE THE RIGHT ADDRESS, DON'T I? HE DOES LIVE HERE, DOESN'T HE?
YES YOU DO AND YES HE DOES...
WAIT HERE AND I'LL SEE IF HE'S IN...

JESUS, THAT WAS DUMB!
I ALMOST GOT A FACE FULL OF MACE!
WHAT DID I GET DRESSED UP LIKE A CAT BURGLAR FOR, ANYWAY?
SLAM

OH GEORGE, THERE'S A FRIEND OF YOURS HERE WHO STOPPED BY TO SEE YOU...
A "FRIEND"? BUT I DON'T...

OH... IT'S YOU...
HEY, OLD PAL! LONG TIME NO SEE!

WELL, THIS CERTAINLY IS A RARE TREAT! I'VE NEVER MET ANY OF GEORGE'S FRIENDS BEFORE...
HAVE A SEAT, BUDDY, AND I'LL GO PUT ON SOME TEA...
NO! DON'T GO!

LOOK, GEORGE, I JUST GOT HOME AND I'VE GOT A MILLION THINGS TO DO! YOU TWO SIT AND GET RE-ACQUAINTED AND I'LL JOIN YOU LATER...
CREAM OR SUGAR, BUDDY?
HUH? OH, BOTH, THANKS!

♪

SO...PRETTY NICE SET-UP, GEORGE. HOW'D YOU EVER SWING SUCH A SWEET DEAL?
NONE OF YOUR BUSINESS. JUST TELL ME WHY YOU'RE HERE AND THEN GO HOME...
SPIN! SPIN!

WHY AM I HERE? YOU MEAN YOU DON'T KNOW? CAN'T YOU EVEN GUESS?
I HAVEN'T THE FOGGIEST NOTION, UNLESS YOU'RE BORED, AND...

THIS IS WHY I'M HERE, "PAL"!
DO YOU KNOW WHAT LIBEL MEANS?
ZYGOTE

...OH... ...THIS... WELL, YOU NEEDN'T TAKE IT PERSONALLY...
...I SIMPLY USED YOU AS A PROTOTYPE, IN ORDER TO ILLUSTRATE A POINT I WAS MAKING...
OH? AND WHAT POINT WAS THAT? THAT PEOPLE LIKE ME OUGHT TO BE EXTERMINATED?!
ZYGOTE

...I'LL INTERPRET YOUR SILENCE AS A "YES"...

HRRUMPH! I CAN SEE YOU'VE ALREADY CONVINCED YOURSELF THAT MY MOTIVES WERE PURELY VINDICTIVE, SO I WON'T WASTE MY TIME BY TRYING TO CONVINCE YOU OTHERWISE...
OH, BUT I'D LIKE TO SEE YOU TRY! I COULD USE A GOOD LAUGH!
GO ON! EXPLAIN TO ME WHY I SHOULDN'T BEAT THE LIVING DAYLIGHTS OUT OF YOU!
TOSS!

LOOK, EVERY WORD I WROTE ABOUT YOU IS TRUE— IF NOT IN FACT AT LEAST IN SPIRIT— AND YOU KNOW IT! YOU SHOULD BE MAD AT YOURSELF, NOT AT ME!
MAYBE YOU WEREN'T FULLY AWARE OF ALL YOUR SHORTCOMINGS BEFORE NOW, BUT NOW YOU ARE, AND YOU SHOULD BE GRATEFUL!

...I NEVER SCREWED LISA WHILE I WAS DATING VAL, YOU KNOW...
...LISA WAS PRETTY UPSET ABOUT THAT...
YEAH, WELL, KNOWING HER, SHE WON'T BE UPSET FOR LONG...

IN FACT, A LOT OF WHAT YOU WROTE ABOUT ME WAS PURE FICTION, AND YOU KNOW IT!
"RUSH LIMBAUGH", GIMME A BREAK!
I ONLY LISTEN TO HIM FOR LAUGHS...

...FORTUNATELY FOR THE BOTH OF US NOBODY READS YOUR STUPID MAGAZINE, OR I'D...
I PRINTED UP 15,000 COPIES...
SHAKE! SHAKE!

WHERE THE HELL DID YOU GET THE MONEY TO PRINT 15,000 COPIES?!? DID SHE GIVE IT TO YOU?!?
LIKE I SAID, IT'S NONE OF YOUR BUSINESS.

OH, I SEE, SHE'S IN ON THIS TOO, HUH?
THAT'S GOOD TO KNOW, 'CUZ THEN I CAN SUE THE BOTH OF YOU, SINCE SHE'S GOT "ASSETS"....LIKE THIS HOUSE, F'RINSTANCE...
SHE HAD NOTHING TO DO WITH IT!

..*SIGH*... OKAY, SHE DID FRONT ME THE MONEY, BUT ONLY BECAUSE SHE BELIEVES IN MY WORK, AND FELT IT DESERVED A WIDER AUDIENCE, SO WE...
WHADAYA MEAN, SHE BELIEVES IN YOUR WORK? DOES SHE THINK SHE'S GONNA GET RICH OFF OF YOU OR SOMETHING?

THAT'S NOT IT AT ALL! SHE... ...SHE...
SHE WHAT?

...SHE THINKS I'M A GENIUS...
HA!!! A "GENIUS"?!? SO IN OTHER WORDS, YOU GET TO LIVE HERE FOR FREE, AND ALL YOU HAVE TO DO IS SIT HERE AND MAKE UP LIES ABOUT ME, WHILE SHE—

THERE'S MORE TO IT THAN THAT! SHE SAYS I GIVE HER LIFE MEANING...AND SUSTENANCE...
YEAH, RIGHT! YOU GIVE HER PUSSY SUSTENANCE, IS MORE LIKE IT...

WHY YOU—
ACK!!!
CHOKE! STRANGLE!

BOYS! BOYS! WHAT ARE YOU DOING!?
BIFF! BAM! KICK! PUNCH!
PUNCH!
GOUGE!

GEORGE, STOP THAT THIS INSTANT! YOU'LL DENT THE FURNITURE!
HUH? ...OH... SORRY...
WHEW! JUST IN TIME! I WAS LOSING!

...I'M SURE THAT WHATEVER IT IS YOU TWO ARE FIGHTING ABOUT COULD BE SETTLED OVER A NICE CUP OF HOT TEA...
I'M AFRAID BUDDY WAS JUST ABOUT TO LEAVE...
OH BOY! 'NILLA WAFERS! MY FAVORITE!

ONE LUMP OR TWO, BUDDY...
TWO, PLEASE...
SAY, NICE CHINA!

THANK YOU. IT WAS A WEDDING GIFT...
"WEDDING"? BUT I—

I'M DIVORCED.. SO TELL ME, ARE YOU THE SAME BUDDY THAT GEORGE WROTE ABOUT IN HIS MAGAZINE? AND IS THAT WHY THE TWO OF YOU ARE QUARRELLING?
WHY, AS A MATTER OF FACT IT IS! HOW PERCEPTIVE OF YOU, WINIFRED!
AT LEAST SOMEONE CAN UNDERSTAND HOW I'M HURTING!

YES, WELL, I TOLD GEORGE IT WAS RATHER... RECKLESS OF HIM TO USE HIS FRIEND'S REAL NAME LIKE THAT...
BUT IT WAS THE TRUTH!!
THE "TRUTH"?!? IT WAS NOTHING BUT LIES! ALL OF IT!!!

HMMM...WELL, WHAT EXACTLY IS THE "TRUTH" IS ALWAYS SUBJECT TO SPECULATION, WHICH IS WHY YOU OUGHT TO FICTIONALIZE YOUR "PROTOTYPES" FROM NOW ON, GEORGE...
SOUND ADVICE!
GRRRRR... I THOUGHT YOU UNDER-STOOD...
SLURP!

YES, I KNOW, "ARTISTIC PURITY" AND ALL THAT, BUT THERE'S A LIMIT TO EVERYTHING...
IF YOU HAD ONLY LISTENED TO ME IN THE FIRST PLACE, NONE OF THIS UNPLEASANTNESS WOULDV'E OCCURRED...
MMMMM... I CAN'T GET ENOUGH OF THESE WAFERS!

SO, SEEING HOW UPSET BUDDY IS OVER ALL OF THIS, I THINK IT'D BE ONLY FAIR THAT YOU ALLOW HIM TO EXPRESS HIS SIDE OF THE STORY IN YOUR NEXT ISSUE...
WHAT?!
NOW THAT'S A GREAT IDEA!

...AND IN FACT I JUST SO HAPPEN TO HAVE A REBUTTAL RIGHT HERE IN MY POCKET, ALL WRITTEN UP AND READY TO GO...
IT SHOULDN'T TAKE UP MORE THAN, OH, SAY, TEN OR FIFTEEN PAGES...
I VERY MUCH DOUBT THAT IT WILL MEET MY EDITORIAL STANDARDS...

OH GEORGE, STOP POUTING! LET'S JUST TRY TO BE CIVIL ABOUT THIS SO THAT WE CAN ALL PROCEED WITH A CLEAN SLATE!
I SWEAR I'VE NEVER SEEN YOU BEHAVE THIS WAY BEFORE, AND I CAN'T SAY THAT I LIKE IT!
(TRUST ME, WINIFRED, YOU AIN'T SEEN NOTHIN'! HE CAN REALLY ACT UP SOMETIMES...)
OKAY, I'LL PRINT IT! NOW CAN WE PLEASE CHANGE THE SUBJECT!

SO TELL ME, HOW DID YOU TWO LOVEBIRDS HAPPEN TO MEET?
OH! WELL, IT WAS AT A SOFTWARE CONVENTION, WHERE I WAS WORKING AS A SALES REP...
I-YI-YI...

...GEORGE WALKED UP TO OUR BOOTH AND BEGAN A RELENTLESS BARRAGE OF, SHALL WE SAY, CHALLENGING QUESTIONS...
NONE OF WHICH YOU COULD ANSWER, BY THE WAY...

...MEANWHILE, I NOTICED HE HAD COPIES OF HIS SELF-PUBLISHED MAGAZINE UNDER HIS ARM, SO OUT OF CURIOSITY I TOOK A FEW HOME AND READ THEM, AND I WAS STRUCK BY THE DEPTH AND ORIGINALITY OF HIS THINKING, ESPECIALLY FOR SOMEONE WITH NO COLLEGE EDUCATION...
"FORMAL" EDUCATION STIFLES ORIGINAL THOUGHT.

...ANYWAY, WE STRUCK UP A CORRESPONDENCE, WHICH EVENTUALLY LED TO MY ASKING GEORGE TO MOVE IN WITH ME...
BOY OH BOY, GEORGE, YOU SURE LUCKED OUT! HERE YOU ARE, LIVING RENT FREE, WITH—
NUDGE! NUDGE!

OH, BUT THAT DOESN'T MATTER! THIS HOUSE WAS PAID OFF YEARS AGO...
BESIDES, GEORGE HELPS ME KEEP THE PLACE UP BY MOWING THE LAWN AND WHAT-NOT...

REALLY? GEORGE MOWS THE LAWN? NOW THAT I'D LIKE TO SEE...
I KNOW WHAT YOU'RE INSINUATING, BUDDY, AND I'D APPRECIATE IT IF YOU'D KEEP YOUR THOUGHTS TO YOURSELF.

"THOUGHTS"? WHAT THOUGHTS? WHAT ARE YOU TALKING ABOUT?
YOU KNOW EXACTLY WHAT I'M TALKING ABOUT, SO DON'T TRY TO BE CUTE!

I SWEAR TO GOD, I HAVE NO IDEA WHAT YOU'RE—
NEITHER DO I, AND I WISH YOU'D STOP IT, GEORGE! ARE YOU ALWAYS THIS HOSTILE TOWARDS YOUR FRIENDS, OR ARE YOU SIMPLY IN A RARE MOOD TODAY?
NEITHER! IT'S JUST THAT I—OH, FORGET IT!

ANYHOW, I OUGHT TO BE GOING...
OH! WELL, IT WAS NICE MEETING YOU, BUDDY! PERHAPS SOME OTHER TIME?
PERHAPS, AND THANKS FOR THE TEA!
WHEW! FINALLY!

...SO YOU WILL BE RUNNING MY REBUTTAL IN YOUR NEXT ISSUE, RIGHT, GEORGE? I DO HAVE YOUR WORD ON THAT...
YES! YES! DON'T PRESS YOUR LUCK!

BY THE WAY, WHAT DID YOU THINK I WAS GOING TO SAY THAT GOT YOU SO UPTIGHT BEFORE?
I THOUGHT YOU WERE GOING TO SAY I WAS "PUSSY-WHIPPED"...

WHAT?! WHY ON EARTH WOULD I SAY THAT? MAN, YOU GOT IT MADE IN THE SHADE! I'M ENVIOUS—
BELIEVE ME, THIS SET-UP ISN'T AS "SWEET" AS YOU SEEM TO THINK IT IS...
SOMETIMES I FEEL LIKE I'M HER PRISONER —OR WORSE, HER PET!

I CAN'T BELIEVE SHE'S GOT ME DOING YARDWORK! IT'S SO... DEMEANING!
JESUS CHRIST! WHAT A PRIMA DONNA!

OH WELL, SO LONG, BUDDY.
YUP. SEE YA.

...OH, UH, GEORGE?
YES?

...YOU MISSED A SPOT, RIGHT OVER HERE...
?!?

VENGEANCE IS MINE!
WHY YOU NGLMM @#@$$!
TA-HA!!

THE END.

MEANWHILE, IN SOME TRENDY LIL "FRISCO" CAFE...

YES, IT IS, ONCE YOU START UNZIPPING YOUR PANTS IN RESTAURANTS—
—NOW WHAT'S THE MATTER?!
SNIFF Y-YOU HATE ME!!! *SOB!*

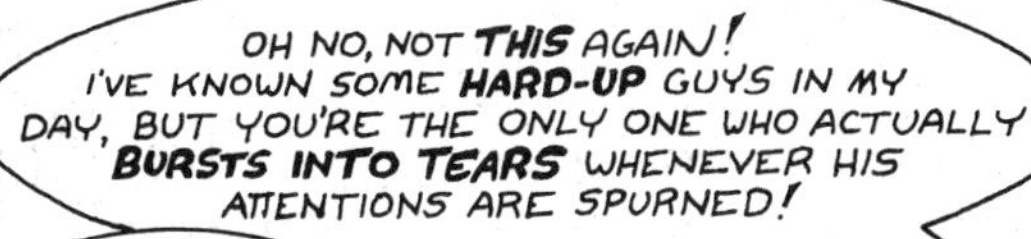

OH NO, NOT THIS AGAIN! I'VE KNOWN SOME HARD-UP GUYS IN MY DAY, BUT YOU'RE THE ONLY ONE WHO ACTUALLY BURSTS INTO TEARS WHENEVER HIS ATTENTIONS ARE SPURNED!
BWÁHHH!!

HEY! WHERE ARE YOU GOING?!
HOME!
AND DON'T BOTHER FOLLOWING ME, 'CAUSE I'VE HAD IT WITH YOU!

B-BUT, CAN'T I AT LEAST GO BACK TO YOUR PLACE SO'S I CAN GATHER ALL MY STUFF?
"STUFF"? WHAT STUFF?! YOU DON'T HAVE ANY STUFF! YOU'VE JUST BEEN MOOCHING OFF OF ME FOR THE LAST MONTH!

AND DON'T TRY TO SWEET TALK YOUR WAY PAST ANY OF MY ROOMMATES EITHER, 'CAUSE THEY ALREADY HATE YOUR GUTS!
...BUT... ...BUT...
GOODBYE, LEONARD!

DARN IT! UNBEKNOWNST TO HER I'VE HID A BAG FULL OF ASSORTED DRUGS UNDER HER MATTRESS THAT I WAS HOARDING FOR MY OWN USE!
I'VE GOT TO FIGURE OUT A WAY TO GET BACK INTO HER PLACE SOMEHOW...
HEY YOU!

WOULD YOU MIND PAYING FOR THESE TWO COFFEES BEFORE YOU LEAVE?
HUH? WHY YES, AS A MATTER OF FACT I WOULD MIND!

YIKES!
WHY YOU NO GOOD @#€3Z...
ZOOM!

LATER...
MAN, IT'S GETTING COLD OUT! AND NOW IT'S STARTING TO RAIN! SHIT!
...WHOEVER WROTE THAT SONG "WARM SAN FRANCISCO NIGHTS" OBVIOUSLY NEVER SET FOOT IN THIS BURG...
BRRRR! I'M GONNA CROAK IF I DON'T WEASEL MY WAY BACK INTO LINDA SUE'S GOOD GRACES, BUT IT'S STILL WAY TOO SOON FOR ME TO GO TO WORK ON HER...
SHE'S SURE TO BE PISSED AT ME FOR AT LEAST A DAY... MAYBE EVEN TWO DAYS... I'VE GOT TO KEEP MY DISTANCE 'TIL THEN OR ELSE I'LL COMPLETELY BLOW IT...
A LEATHER JACKET!
CHATTER! CHATTER!
A NON-CONFORM-IST!
NOW THINK...THERE MUST BE SOME-ONE I KNOW WHO LIVES AROUND HERE THAT I COULD CRASH WITH...
PREFERABLY FEMALE...
TAP! TAP!
I SHOULD CHECK THESE SCRAPS OF PAPER AND MATCHBOOK COVERS I'VE GOT IN MY POCKET...
THERE OUGHT TO BE A USEFUL PHONE NUMBER OR ADDRESS ON AT LEAST ONE OF 'EM...
AH HA, HERE'S ONE! "TRACY"...YEAH, I REMEMBER HER...
AND SHE ONLY LIVES ABOUT 20 BLOCKS FROM HERE... MIGHT AS WELL GIVE HER A CALL...
—WHOA, WHAT'S THIS?
...IT'S THAT UNUSED ONE-WAY TICKET TO NEW YORK THAT THAT DRUNKEN CARTOONIST GAVE ME LAST WEEK, AND IT LEAVES TOMORROW!
I FORGOT ALL ABOUT THIS!
EE-YES! THIS TICKET IS LIKE A GIFT FROM THE HEAVENS! AT LAST I CAN GET AWAY FROM THIS DRIPPY HIPPY DISNEYLAND!
NEW YORK IS THE ONLY PLACE FOR AN AMBITIOUS GUY LIKE ME, AND IT'S ABOUT TIME I WENT BACK TO STAKE MY CLAIM!
LOOK AT ME! I'M CRAZY!
CLICK!
BUT MEANWHILE, I'D BETTER CALL THIS TRACY CHICK BEFORE I CATCH PNEUMONIA...
MAYBE SHE COULD GIVE ME A LIFT TO THE AIRPORT TOMORROW, TOO...

DRAT! SHE'S NOT HOME YET!
BUT I MIGHT AS WELL START WALKING TOWARDS HER PLACE ANY WAY...
IT'S NOT LIKE I HAVE A CHOICE...
SLAM!

AN HOUR LATER...
WHEW! THESE HILLS ARE INSANE!
...AND SHE LIVES FARTHER AWAY THAN I THOUGHT ...I'M NOT TOO SURE I'M GONNA MAKE IT...
AND WHAT IF SHE'S STILL NOT HOME WHEN I GET THERE?
JESUS...

I WISH I COULD JUST JUMP INTO ONE OF THESE CARS THAT KEEP ZOOMING BY...
YOU'D THINK AT LEAST SOME LONELY OLD HOMO WOULD STOP AND OFFER ME A RIDE...
...MAYBE BUY ME DINNER... AND PROVIDE ME WITH MY OWN APARTMENT...

—NOW THERE'S AN IDEA! I SHOULD TRY A LITTLE HUSTLING!
HELL, I AIN'T PROUD! PLUS I KNOW LOTS OF GUYS WHO'VE DONE THIS WHEN TIMES ARE TOUGH! IT'S NO BIG DEAL!
I'LL JUST STAND HERE FOR A WHILE AND WAIT FOR A POTENTIAL CUSTOMER TO PASS MY WAY...

ANOTHER HOUR LATER...
SHIT! IT'S POURING OUT NOW! WON'T SOMEONE AT LEAST STOP OUT OF SYMPATHY?!
WHAT'S THE MATTER, AIN'T I GOOD ENOUGH FOR YOU BASTARDS?!
ZIP!
ZOOM!

AAH, FUCK IT! I MIGHT AS WELL KEEP WALKING...
AT LEAST I STILL GOT MY PRIDE, FOR WHAT THAT'S WORTH...
AND AT THE MOMENT THAT AIN'T MUCH...
TRUDGE! TRUDGE!

EVENTUALLY...
AH, GOOD! HER LIGHTS ARE ON, SO SHE MUST BE HOME...
HOPEFULLY SHE PLAYED MY MESSAGE AND IS EXPECTING ME...

ONLY SHE'S NOT GONNA BE TOO IMPRESSED WITH ME, CONSIDERING THE CONDITION I'M IN...
I MUST LOOK LIKE THE BEGGAR THAT I AM...

—THAT'S IT! I'LL PLAY UP MY DESPERATE SITUATION TO THE Nth DEGREE...
THAT WAY SHE'LL FEEL SO SORRY FOR ME SHE'LL HAVE TO TAKE ME IN!
BZZZT!
BANG!

...WOMEN ARE USUALLY TURNED-OFF BY DESPERATE TYPES, BUT YOU CAN ALWAYS APPEAL TO THEIR MATERNAL INSTINCTS IF YOU PLAY YOUR CARDS RIGHT...
KNOCK! KNOCK!

HI, LEONARD! I JUST GOT YOUR...
LEONARD?
UGGGHHH...

OHMIGOD! LEONARD, WHAT'S WRONG?!
PLOP!

THE NEXT DAY...
THAT SURE WAS NICE OF TRACY TO PUT ME UP, AND GIVE ME A LIFT TO THE AIRPORT, AND FEED ME CHICKEN SOUP 'TIL IT CAME OUT OF MY EARS 'N' STUFF...
I SHOULD HOLD ON TO HER ADDRESS, JUST IN CASE...

...NOT THAT I EVER INTEND TO MOVE BACK TO "FRISCO", NO-SIR-REE-BOB...
I'VE GOT A FEELING THAT THINGS ARE GONNA GO REAL WELL FOR ME IN NEW YORK THIS TIME...
DOING WHAT I DON'T KNOW, BUT THAT'S BESIDES THE POINT AT THE MOMENT...

...MAN, I LOVE FLYING ON AIRPLANES... ESPECIALLY ON A CLEAR DAY LIKE TODAY...
WISH I WAS ON ACID RIGHT NOW — WAIT, DIDN'T I JUST SCORE SOME LAST WEEK? I COULD'A SWORN I...

OH NO! MY STASH!!!
?
!

THE END.

"THE OLD FLAME"
STARRING: BUDDY BRADLEY!
©1993
BY PETER BAGGE
UMPF!
WUMP!
HEAVE!

WHOA...
EASY, BOY, EASY...

IT SEEMS LIKE MY LAUNDRY KEEPS GETTING HEAVIER ALL THE TIME...
...AND THE TRIP TO THE LAUNDROMAT KEEPS GETTING LONGER AND LONGER...

* SIGH *... THIS WEEKLY RITUAL NEVER FAILS TO REMIND ME OF MY LOWLY ECONOMIC STATUS...
...AND WHAT LUXURY IT WOULD BE TO OWN A SIMPLE, PLAIN OLD WASHING MACHINE...
...AS WELL AS OWNING A HOME I COULD PUT IT IN...
...TRUDGE, TRUDGE, TRUDGE...
LAUNDRO

ARRGH. CROWDED, AS USUAL.

UH-OH, I THINK THIS IS THE MACHINE THAT ALWAYS GOES HAYWIRE ON ME...
BUT IT'S THE ONLY ONE AVAILABLE, AND I DON'T FEEL LIKE WAITING...

OH WELL, HERE GOES NOTHING...
PLEASE DON'T CRAP OUT ON ME, MACHINE...

KICK!
!?!

WHAT WAS THAT? WHO KICKED ME?! WHO—

HI!
!?! OH, UH, HI! W-WHAT ARE YOU DOING HERE?!

WASHING MY CLOTHES, SAME AS YOU...
NO, I MEAN, I THOUGHT YOU WERE IN FRANCE...

OH, I'VE BEEN BACK FOR MONTHS! THAT TRIP WAS ONLY TEMPORARY...
MONTHS?! THEN HOW COME I HAVEN'T SEEN YOU AROUND? HAVE YOU BEEN TRYING TO AVOID ME?

NO, NOT AT ALL! IT'S JUST THAT I'VE BEEN HANGING OUT WITH A DIFFERENT CROWD LATELY...
I, UH, WAS INVOLVED WITH AN OLDER GUY FOR A WHILE...
OH YEAH? WHO? YOUR BOSS?

OH, IT'S A LONG STORY... I'LL TELL YOU ALL ABOUT IT SOME OTHER TIME...
AH-HA! I KNEW SHE WAS BANGING HER BOSS!

IN FACT, I'VE INVITED SOME OLD FRIENDS OVER FOR DINNER TOMORROW NIGHT, AND IF YOU'D LIKE TO COME TOO YOU'RE MORE THAN WELCOME...
TOMORROW NIGHT, HUH? HMM... SOUNDS LIKE FUN, ONLY...
ONLY WHAT?

WELL... IT'S JUST THAT I'VE BEEN KINDA GOING OUT WITH LISA, LATELY...
SO I'VE HEARD..., I HEARD YOU'RE LIVING WITH HER AS WELL...

...UH... ...YEAH... THAT TOO...
WELL, SHE'S WELCOME TO COME, TOO, UNLESS YOU THINK THAT'LL BE TOO WEIRD...
SCRATCH! SCRATCH!

WELL, I'LL ASK HER, BUT IF SHE DOESN'T WANT TO GO I'LL JUST COME BY MYSELF...
I MEAN, IF THAT'S OKAY WITH YOU...
SURE, THAT'S FINE!

..SO... I GUESS I OWE YOU AN APOLOGY...
AN APOLOGY? FOR WHAT?

FOR DISAPPEARING FROM YOUR LIFE WITHOUT A WORD OF EXPLANATION...
...OH... ...THAT... WELL, I JUST SORTA FIG-URED—

IT JUST SEEMED OBVIOUS THAT THINGS WERE GONNA GET UGLY BETWEEN US, AND I DIDN'T LIKE THE WAY I WAS TURNING INTO A SHREW...
GUESS THAT WAS PRETTY UN-FAIR OF ME, HUH?
NAH... IT WAS UNDER-STANDABLE...
DAMN STRAIGHT IT WAS UNFAIR!

...AND THEN WHEN I HEARD THAT THINGS DIDN'T WORK OUT FOR YOU AS A BAND MANAGER I FELT TERRIBLE, LIKE I WAS RESPONSIBLE SOMEHOW...
OH, DON'T BE SILLY...I WAS BOUND TO GET OUT OF THAT BUSINESS EVENTUALLY...
GOOD! I'M GLAD YOU FELT TERRIBLE!
MEANWHILE, THINGS HAVEN'T PANNED OUT TOO WELL FOR ME, EITHER...
PARIS WAS GREAT, BUT AS YOU GUESSED I DID WIND UP GETTING ROMANTICALLY INVOLVED WITH MY EMPLOYER, WHICH MADE THINGS RATHER AWKWARD FOR ME, JOB-WISE...
I COULD WELL IMAGINE...
SLUT!

SO ONCE WE GOT BACK I QUIT, AND I'VE BEEN LOOKING FOR A NEW JOB EVER SINCE...
...PLUS PAUL AND I HAVEN'T BEEN GETTING ALONG TOO WELL LATELY, SO NOW I HAVE TO FIND MY OWN PLACE BEFORE HE GETS BACK FROM A BUSINESS TRIP, WHICH IS TWO WEEKS FROM NOW...
GEE, THAT'S A TOUGH BREAK...
YOU DESERVE IT, YOU TRAMP!
ANYHOW, THAT'S WHY I'M THROWING MY DINNER PARTY THIS WEEK— MIGHT AS WELL SHOW OFF MY FABULOUS LIVING SPACE WHILE I'M STILL LIVING THERE, RIGHT?
MIGHT AS WELL, HEH-HEH...
THAT'S RIGHT, TAKE ADVANTAGE OF THE OLD FART WHILE HE'S OUT OF TOWN, YOU WHORE!

OOPS, MY LAUNDRY'S DONE... HERE'S THE ADDRESS, AND DINNER'S AT EIGHT...
HOPE TO SEE YOU THEN!
DON'T WORRY, I'LL BE THERE...
'BYE, BUDDY! NICE TO SEE YOU AGAIN!
LIKE-WISE!
...I'M IN LOVE...
THUMP! THUMP! THUMP!

THE NEXT DAY...

...I'LL SEE YOU LATER, LISA... I'M, UH, HEADING OVER TO PHIL'S TO DUB SOME RECORDS...
UH-HUH... SO YOU TOLD ME...
...THIS IS JEOPARDY!...

...AND AFTER THAT I MAY GET TOGETHER WITH SOME OF THE GUYS FOR A BEER, SO DON'T EXPECT ME HOME TOO SOON...
OKAY, SO GO ALREADY! I'M TRYING TO HEAR MY SHOW!

WHEW! THAT WAS EASY!
BUT THEN, WHY SHOULD SHE SUSPECT ANYTHING? AFTER ALL, I REALLY AM GOING OVER TO PHIL'S... FIRST, ANYWAY...

I HOPE PHIL DOESN'T CATCH ON TO WHAT I'M UP TO, 'CUZ HE'S LIKELY TO SPILL THE BEANS TO LISA...
I'VE GOT TO BE CAREFUL OF WHAT I DO OR SAY...

LATER...

HEY PHIL, WHAT'S WITH ALL THE PRANK PHONE CALL TAPES? ARE YOU INTO THIS SORT OF THING?
NOT REALLY, BUT PEOPLE KEEP GIVING 'EM TO ME ANYWAY...
I USED TO HATE YA...
LOUVIN BROS

...IF YOU ASK ME THEY'RE ALL RATHER WITLESS AND CRUEL...PLUS ONCE YOU'VE HEARD ONE YOU'VE PRETTY MUCH HEARD 'EM ALL...
BUT IF YOU'RE INTO 'EM FEEL FREE TO TAKE 'EM...THEY'RE ALL YOURS...
UHH, NO THANKS. YOUR ASSESSMENT OF THEM HAS SOURED ME ON THEM FOREVER...

SAY, UH, WOULD YOU MIND IF I USE YOUR BATHROOM TO, LIKE, SHAVE 'N' STUFF?
HUH? OH, NO, GO AHEAD...

...OUR PLUMBING IS ON THE FRITZ...

ONCE I'M DONE TAPING THIS ALBUM I'LL BE ON MY WAY AND OUT OF YOUR HAIR...
TAKE YOUR TIME, I DON'T HAVE ANY PLANS...

SSSPROCK!

SO, BUDDY, DID YOU HEAR THAT VALERIE IS BACK IN TOWN?
SCOPE

HUH? OH, UH, YES, I THINK I HEARD SOMETHING TO THAT EFFECT...
WHY, DID YOU HEAR FROM HER RECENTLY?
YEAH, SHE CALLED ME UP THE OTHER DAY TO INVITE ME TO SOME LITTLE DINNER PARTY SHE'S THROWING, BUT I DECLINED...
I SORTA HAVE MIXED FEELINGS ABOUT HER...

OH, THAT'S RIGHT, DIDN'T THE TWO OF YOU HAVE SOMETHING GOING A LONG TIME AGO?
DID SHE TELL YOU THAT? OH JEEZ, I WISH SHE WOULDN'T DO THAT...
SCOPE

WHY? ARE YOU EMBARRASSED ABOUT THAT?
WELL, YEAH, KINDA... I DUNNO...
...WE STARTED OUT AS JUST GOOD PALS, BUT AT A CERTAIN POINT SHE BEGAN TO MAKE IT OBVIOUS THAT SHE WANTED TO BE MORE THAN THAT...

SIGH... I GUESS THE IDEA OF HAVING A "GIRLFRIEND" STILL HAD SOME APPEAL TO ME AT THE TIME...
PLUS SHE'S AWFULLY DETERMINED TO GET HER OWN WAY, AS I'M SURE YOU KNOW... I WAS ACTUALLY AFRAID TO SAY NO TO HER...

OH GOD, WHAT A MISTAKE! WHAT ON EARTH WAS I THINK-ING?...
HEY NOW, WAIT A MINUTE! VALERIE'S A FINE LOOKING WOMAN! I DON'T SEE WHAT YOU HAVE TO BE ASHAMED OF...

BUT THAT'S JUST IT, BUDDY— SHE'S A GIRL! I MEAN, JESUS CHRIST...
JUST THINKING ABOUT TRYING TO "GET IT ON" WITH HER MAKES ME CRINGE...

...NO OFFENSE, BUT PUSSIES REALLY GROSS ME OUT...

TEN MINUTES LATER...
WELP, I GUESS I'LL BE ON MY WAY... HEH-HEH...
?!? WHAT ARE YOU ALL SPRUCED UP FOR?!?

WAIT A MINUTE, THIS DOESN'T HAVE ANYTHING TO DO WITH VALERIE, DOES IT?
DON'T TELL ME YOU GOT INVITED TO HER PARTY TOO! IS THAT WHERE YOU'RE GOING? HMM? IS THAT WHAT THIS IS ALL ABOUT?
DON'T TELL LISA...

GOOD LORD! I DON'T BELIEVE IT!
YOU'RE A SICK MAN, BUDDY! A SICK, TWISTED, DEPRAVED...
HEY MAN, IT'S NOT WHAT YOU THINK!
SLAP!

SHE SIMPLY INVITED ME OVER FOR DINNER, AND THAT'S ALL!
BESIDES, IT'S A PARTY! SO WHAT COULD POSSIBLY HAPPEN WITH ALL THOSE OTHER PEOPLE AROUND, HMM? WHAT?!
OKAY, YOU MADE YOUR POINT...

...AND I APOLOGIZE FOR GETTING ON YOUR CASE, BUT I STILL THINK THIS IS A DANGEROUS THING YOUR DOING...
FEH. WHERE'S THE DANGER?

WELL, ARE YOU STILL IN LOVE WITH HER?
W-WHO, ME?! NO WAY!

SIGH VERY WELL THEN, PROCEED AT YOUR OWN RISK...
AND DON'T WORRY, I WON'T SAY ANYTHING TO LISA...
IS THAT A PROMISE? I JUST DON'T WANT HER FLIPPING OUT OVER NOTHING...

I PROMISE! I PROMISE! STOP EXPLAINING YOURSELF! HAVE A BLAST, SEE IF I CARE!
THANKS, MAN! THANKS FOR EVERYTHING!
GOTTA SPLIT—SEE YA!

SLAM!

..AAH, HE'S STILL IN LOVE...
THE AQUA-VELVA GAVE HIM AWAY...

LATER...
...LOOKS LIKE ONE OF THOSE FANCY-SHMANCY, RENOVATED LOFT-SPACES...
THIS MUST BE THE PLACE, I RECKON...
...I ALWAYS FORGET THAT PEOPLE ACTUALLY LIVE IN THESE BUILDINGS...
2605
LET'S GET PRIMITIVE ART GALLERY
...I USED TO LIVE IN ONE, THOUGH IT WAS NOTHING LIKE THIS...

NOW LET'S SEE... "WEBSTER" IS HER BOYFRIEND'S LAST NAME...
WHAT A STUCK-UP, WASPY-ISH SOUNDING NAME...
BZZZT!

HMMM... GUESS I HAVE TO TAKE THE ELEVATOR UP...
HOPE IT DOESN'T GET STUCK ON ME...
I HATE ELEVATORS...
BUZZZ!

ONLY A TOTAL YUPPIE WITH A NAME LIKE "WEBSTER" WOULD LIVE IN A CREEPY PLACE LIKE THIS...
I'M STARTING TO HAVE DOUBTS ABOUT COMING TO THIS THING...

NOW WHICH WAY? I'M TOTALLY CONFUSED...
OH, HERE IT IS, RIGHT IN FRONT OF ME...
3B
* GULP! * GUESS THERE'S NO TURNING BACK NOW...

KNOCK! KNO—
YES?
3B
OH! HI, I'M LOOKING FOR V—

HEY VAL! LOOKS LIKE ANOTHER GUEST HAS ARRIVED!
3B
I DON'T THINK I LIKE THIS PERSON...

BUDDY, YOU MADE IT! I'M SO GLAD!
H-HI, VALERIE...

LEMME SEE WHAT YOU BROUGHT WITH YOU...
OMIGOD, "BALLARD BITTER"! STILL ADDICTED, I SEE...
I..GUESS...I'VE GIVEN UP CIGS, THOUGH. IT'S BEEN TWO WHOLE WEEKS...

GOOD! GOOD FOR YOU...
C'MON, I'LL INTRODUCE YOU TO EVERY-ONE...
UHH, CAN I HAVE ONE OF MY BEERS, PLEASE?

ALICE, RAYMOND, THIS IS MY OLD FRIEND, BUDDY!
NOW YOU GUYS TALK WHILE I GO CHECK ON THE DINNER...
HI.
HI.
HIYA!

SWIG!

ITCH! ITCH!
SCRATCH! SCRATCH!
?
WIPE!

—ALICE, WHERE'S THE SALAD? DIDN'T YOU MAKE IT ALREADY?
UH...NO, I...
ITCH! ITCH!

WELL YOU'D BETTER GET TO WORK ON IT, DON'T YOU THINK?!
...I... UHHH...
SHAKE! SHAKE!
!

RAYMOND, GO HELP ALICE MAKE THE SALAD...
...BUDDY, YOU COME WITH ME...
HUH?
?
YANK!

...SO WHAT DO YOU THINK OF THIS PLACE, BUDDY? PRETTY FANCY, HUH?
I GUESS, THOUGH IT SURE AIN'T TO MY TASTE...

...ALL THESE ZIG-ZAGGY TABLES AND ART OBJECTS MAKE ME A LITTLE NERVOUS...
A PERSON COULD GET HURT IF THEY DON'T WATCH WHERE THEY'RE GOING...
YES, WELL, PAUL KNOWS ALL THESE ARTISTS PERSONALLY, AND BUYS DIRECTLY FROM THEM...
ALL THIS STUFF WOULD COST A FORTUNE IF YOU BOUGHT IT THROUGH A GALLERY...

TO BE PERFECTLY HONEST, I'M GOING TO MISS LIVING HERE...
...I'VE GROWN SORT OF ATTACHED TO SOME OF THE PIECES IN PAUL'S COLLECTION...
REALLY? LIKE WHICH ONES?

OH, LIKE THAT PAINTING OVER THERE, F'RINSTANCE...
I THINK IT'S A REAL POWERFUL PIECE...
WHICH PAINTING? WHERE?

THAT ONE.
THAT ONE?!? OY! ...QUICK, LET'S CHANGE THE SUBJECT...

LATER...

OH, BUDDY, I NEVER FINISHED INTRODUCING YOU TO EVERYONE, HAVE I?
...WELL, SITTING NEXT TO YOU IS MY NEW BEST FRIEND, ELLEN!
HI.
HI-I-I-I, ♪ BUDDY... ♪

...I'VE HEARD AN AWFUL LOT ABOUT YOU, "LOVER-BOY"... TEE-HEE!
HEH-HEH...
YIKES!

...AND SITTING ACROSS FROM YOU IS NIGEL AND IAN, WHOM I MADE A POINT OF INVITING SINCE THEY SHARE YOUR INTEREST IN MUSIC FROM THE '60s...
YEAH, I COULD TELL BY THE WAY YOU GUYS ARE DRESSED THAT YOU MUST BE HEAVILY INTO THE BEATLES 'N' STUFF LIKE THAT...
...THE... "BEATLES"?
SNICKER!
BASS ALE

YEAH, THE BEATLES! WHAT, DID I COMMIT SOME KIND OF FAUX PAS BY MENTIONING THEM OR SOMETHING?
N-NO, WE LIKE THE BEATLES...

IAN AND NIGEL ARE BOTH ORIGINALLY FROM NEW JERSEY, TOO, BY THE WAY...
YA DON'T SAY! WHAT PART OF JERSEY ARE YOU GUYS FROM?

...WELL?!
W-WHAT'S WITH THE THIRD DEGREE, MAN?

* AHEM *...
AND SITTING BENEATH YOU, BUDDY, IS MY GOOD FRIEND GUNTER...
WHAT TH—
HALLO!

GUNTER'S FROM GERMANY, BUT HE LIKES TO VISIT SEATTLE BECAUSE HE'S INTO "GRUNGE"...
NOT SO! DAT VAS LAST YEAR! DIS YEAR I'M ON MY WAY TO OLYMPIA, VITCH HASS A MUCH MORE HAPPENING SCENE THAN ZEATTLE DOES! ZEATTLE ISS HISTORY! ZEATTLE ISS A JOKE!
WHY ARE YOU SITTING UNDER MY CHAIR?

OH, I'M NOT VERY HUNGRY...
I JUST VANT TO MAKE LIKE A FLY ON ZEE WALL UND— VAT ISS ZEE WORD?— "EAVESDROP"...
HEH-HEH...

...DAT REMINDS ME, VALERIE— VERE ISS MY ALKA-ZELTZER? MINE STOMACH ISS NOT FEELINK SO GOOD...
OH! THAT'S RIGHT, I FORGOT...
ALICE! BRING ALKA-SELTZER, PLEASE!

...UH, VALERIE, RAYMOND AND I WHERE WONDERING IF WPSSPSSP-PSSTPS—
?
AFTER DINNER, ALICE.
DANKE...

UH, YEAH, BUT PSST. PSSPRm
ONCE DINNER IS OVER AND THE TABLE IS CLEARED THEN YOU CAN GO SHOOT UP! CAN'T YOU AND RAYMOND WAIT UNTIL THEN?

CAN YOU BELIEVE THE TWO OF THEM?! LIKE THEY CAN'T WAIT ANOTHER TWENTY MINUTES!
I MEAN, REALLY...
* GIGGLE!*
I... UH...
WHAT THE HELL IS GOING ON AROUND HERE?

ONE HOUR AND SIX BREWED-TO-PERFECTION BALLARD BITTERS LATER...

...SO, WHAT EXACTLY IS THE STORY WITH THIS EX-BOSS/EX-BOYFRIEND OF YOURS? HOW'D YOU WIND UP DATING HIM IN THE FIRST PLACE?
HOW? WELL, WHAT CAN I SAY... PAUL'S A VERY SPECIAL PERSON...
I'VE NEVER MET ANYONE QUITE LIKE HIM BEFORE...

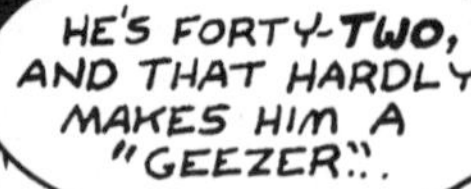

YEAH, BUT HOW OLD IS HE, FORTY? WHAT DO YOU WANT FROM AN OLD GEEZER LIKE THAT?
HE'S FORTY-TWO, AND THAT HARDLY MAKES HIM A "GEEZER."

FEH. IF YOU ASK ME THERE MUST BE SOMETHING SERIOUSLY WRONG WITH HIM TO GO CHASING AFTER A YOUNG CHICK LIKE YOU... IT'S UNDIGNIFIED...
...TELL ME, HAVE YOU CONSIDERED SUING HIM?
SUING HIM? FOR WHAT?
SPIN
LATEST ODD-LOOKING BANDS FROM ENGLAND.
ICE-CUBE: "I'LL SMASH YOUR HONKY FACE IN..."
MORE AIDS HYSTERIA FOR YOU TO SWEAT OVER
DISAPPOINTING RESULTS OF READERS POLL
ABSOLUT NORFLU...

FOR SEXUAL HARASSMENT! AFTER ALL, HE WAS YOUR BOSS AT THE TIME, RIGHT?
OH FOR GOODNESS SAKES, BUDDY! IT WASN'T LIKE THAT AT ALL...
THOUGH I MUST ADMIT YOU'RE NOT THE FIRST PERSON TO MAKE THAT SUGGESTION...

THERE, YA SEE?! WHO CARES WHAT THE CIRCUMSTANCES WERE! HE SHOULD BE PUNISHED SIMPLY FOR BEING A DIRTY OLD MAN!
IF HE WAS HERE I'D KICK HIS ASS IN TWO SECONDS FLAT...
PAUL'S SIX FOOT THREE...

SO WHAT?! HE'S OLD, ISN'T HE?! HE'S AN OLD, BROKEN-DOWN, DECREPIT...
I DON'T CONSIDER FORTY-TWO TO BE ALL THAT OLD, EITHER...

HUH? WHAT DID YOU SAY?!?
N-N-NOTHING...

HEY, HOW COME YOU GUYS DON'T TALK WITH FAKE BRITISH ACCENTS AND SAY "FAB" AND "GEAR" AND SHIT LIKE THAT, HMMM?.
IT SEEMS TO ME LIKE YOUR WHOLE SHTICK ISN'T COMPLETE WITHOUT IT, Y'KNOW WHAT I'M SAYIN'?

WELL?!?

I-I DUNNO... TH-THAT WOULD BE RATHER PRETENTIOUS, OF US, DON'T YOU THINK?
TEE-HEE *GIGGLE!*

AND WHAT ARE YOU GIGGLING ABOUT ALL THE TIME?!
GASP!

WELL?!?

SOB
?

THAT DOES IT. I'M OUTTA HERE...
S'CUSE ME, GUNTER...
SNIFFLE *CHOKE*...
WAIT, BUDDY! DON'T GO YET!

BUT, I...
(JUST COME INTO THE KITCHEN SO WE CAN TALK ALONE FOR A SEC, OKAY?)
WAAAH!
ACH, ALL THIS ARGUING ISS MAKING MINE STOMACH FEEL EFAN VORSE...
MORE ALKA-ZELTZER, PLEASE!

LOOK, VAL, I'M SORRY ABOUT THE WAY I WAS PUTTING DOWN YOUR BOYFRIEND BEFORE... ...THAT WAS PRETTY UNCALLED FOR...
OH, THAT'S OKAY—HE'S NOT MY BOYFRIEND ANYMORE, REMEMBER?

BESIDES, IT TOLD ME THAT YOU STILL "CARE", AT LEAST A LITTLE BIT... AM I RIGHT?
UH, WELL, YEAH... I SUPPOSE...
BUT STILL, I'M AFRAID I OFFENDED YOUR GUESTS...

DON'T WORRY ABOUT IT! I KNEW MY FRIENDS WOULD GET ON YOUR NERVES, WHICH IS PARTLY WHY I INVITED YOU...
SHOVE!
OOF!
REALLY? I DON'T—

I WAS HOPING YOU'D GET DRUNK AND START SCREAMING AT PEOPLE THE WAY YOU DID...
IT SORT OF REMINDED ME OF OLD TIMES...
OH, WELL, I...(GULP!)...

LOOK, BUDDY, I, UH, DON'T WANT TO CAUSE ANY TROUBLE... I JUST FELT LIKE... HANGING OUT WITH YOU ONE MORE TIME...
IS THAT OKAY? FOR OLD TIMES SAKE?
SH-SH-SURE... I DON'T HAVE A PROBLEM WITH THAT...

J-JEEZUS, VAL, YOU SURE GOT SKINNY...
HA! I WISH... I'D STILL LIKE TO LOSE ANOTHER TEN POUNDS...

ANOTHER TEN POUNDS? BUT...WHY?!? YOU WERE JUST RIGHT BACK WHEN WE WERE GOIN' OUT...
OH GOD, I WAS A FAT PIG BACK THEN! I DON'T KNOW HOW YOU COULD STAND TO BE SEEN WITH ME AT THE TIME!

SMOOOCH!
OMIGOSH! WE'RE KISSING! ONLY... IT DOESN'T QUITE FEEL THE SAME AS IT USETA...
PLUS, SHE'S SO DAMNED SCRAWNY NOW! SHE'S JUST SKIN 'N' BONE!

...UGH, EVEN HER ASS CHEEKS FEEL BONEY! GROSS!
...BUT I DON'T DARE TAKE MY HAND AWAY OR SHE'LL BE INSULTED...
SMOOCH! SLOBBER! KISS!

—YIKES!
WHAT IS IT? WHAT'S THE MATTER?

LOOK!
OH, THEY'RE OKAY...THEY'RE JUST NODDING OUT...
JUST ACT LIKE THEY'RE NOT EVEN THERE...

UH, LOOK, I REALLY SHOULD GO...
AWW, MUST YOU? I'M SORRY IF ALICE AND RAYMOND UPSET YOU...
THEY'RE REALLY QUITE HARMLESS...

I BELIEVE YOU, ONLY I DIDN'T INTEND TO STAY OUT THIS LATE, AND I DON'T WANT LISA TO GET SUSPICIOUS...
OKAY... I UNDERSTAND...

ANYHOW, IT WAS NICE SEEING YOU AGAIN, AND THANKS FOR STOPPING BY...
IT WAS MY PLEASURE, AND THANKS FOR THE DINNER...
OH, BUDDY...

...I VAS VONDERING IF YOU HAFF ANY FRIENDS OR CONNECTIONS DOWN IN OLYMPIA...
"CONNECTIONS"? WHY?

BECAUSE I VAS GOING TO ESK YOU IF YOU'D LIKE TO ACCOMPANY ME WHEN I GO DOWN THERE TOMORROW, AND PERHAPS ACT AS MY GUIDE...
NO!!

SLAM!
?

LATER...
SO, HOW'S VALERIE DOING?
OH, MAN, DON'T ASK. SHE'S—

WHAT?!? HOW DID YOU KNOW?! DON'T TELL ME—
PHIL TOLD ME EVERYTHING! I FORCED IT OUT OF HIM!
YOU GOT A LOT OF NERVE, SNEAKING AROUND BEHIND MY BACK!...

OKAY, CALM DOWN, I CONFESS, I DID GO TO HER LITTLE PARTY...
BUT BELIEVE ME, YOU HAD NOTHING TO WORRY ABOUT...
SO WHO SAYS I'M WORRIED?

I'M TELLIN' YA, LISA, YOU WOULD NOT BELIEVE WHAT A SELF-OBSESSED, ANOREXIC TRENDOID SHE'S BECOME...
AND HER FRIENDS—OY! WHAT A BUNCH OF INSECURE POSEURS!
I KNOW, I'VE SEEN 'EM...

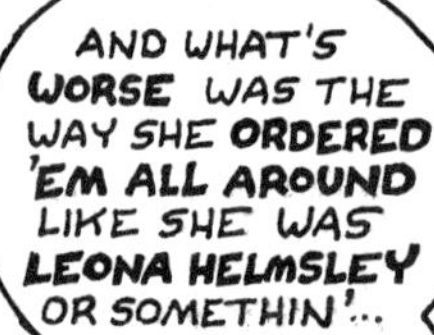

AND WHAT'S WORSE WAS THE WAY SHE ORDERED 'EM ALL AROUND LIKE SHE WAS LEONA HELMSLEY OR SOMETHIN'...
IT WAS FRIGHTENING, THE WAY SHE WALKED ALL OVER THEM!
I COULD WELL IMAGINE...

IT MADE ME REALIZE FOR THE FIRST TIME HOW LUCKY I AM THAT SHE DUMPED ME...
OTHERWISE MY LIFE COULD BE A LIVING HELL RIGHT NOW...
I COULDA TOLD YOU THAT ALL ALONG...

SIGH ANYHOW, I'M SORRY I DIDN'T TELL YOU UP FRONT WHERE I WAS GOING...
I JUST DIDN'T WANT YOU TO GET ALL MAD OVER NOTHING...
OH, I'M NOT REALLY MAD. JUST TRY NOT TO BE SUCH A WEASEL NEXT TIME, OKAY?
OKAY...
UH, I'M GONNA TAKE A SHOWER NOW...

SLAM!
WIGLET

WHEW!
WIGLET

END.

STINKY DOES GOTHAM.
© 1993
BY P. BAGGE
ZZZZZZ...
DIAL, DIAL, DIAL...

RING! RING! RING—
HELLO?
(HELLO, CONNIE? THIS IS LEONARD)...
ZZZZz...

"LEONARD"? ...OH, HI! WHY ARE YOU WHISPERING?
(BECAUSE, I'M, UH, CALLING FROM A CHURCH...
(LISTEN, WOULD YOU MIND IF I CRASHED AT YOUR PLACE FOR A FEW MONTHS?)...

A FEW MONTHS?!? YOU GOTTA BE KIDDING!
ALL RIGHT, A FEW WEEKS THEN! THAT'S ALL I'M ASKING!
WHAT'S THE BIG DEAL? I THOUGHT YOU LIKED ME?

I DO LIKE YOU, LEONARD, ONLY I'M AFRAID IT SIMPLY ISN'T POSSIBLE...
WELL, THEN, THINK OF MY STAY AS A VACATION! YOU KNOW ME, I'M MR. PARTY GUY!
I DON'T HAVE A VERY BIG PLACE, AND WE'RE OVER-CROWDED AS IT IS...
THERE'S NEVER A DULL MOMENT WHEN I'M AROUND, RIGHT?
AM I RIGHT OR WHAT?

WELL, I...
OY VEY! WHY WAS I EVER NICE TO THIS GUY?!
YOU KNOW IT'S TRUE! STICK WITH ME AND I'LL GET YOU INTO ALL THE CLUBS FOR FREE! I'VE DONE IT BE-FORE, HAVEN'T I?
WHADAYA SAY, DO WE HAVE A DEAL? CAN I CRASH WITH YOU OR NO?

ERRRRR... WELL...
I'VE GOT HER NOW! HEH, HEH, HEH...

...NO.
WHAT?!? WHY YOU—
...LEONARD?

OOPS!
SLAM!
OH, HI, LORI! I DIDN'T KNOW YOU WERE AWAKE!
WHO WAS THAT ON THE PHONE?

WHA? WHO? OH, UH, I WAS JUST RECONFIRMING MY AUDITION FOR THIS AFTERNOON, THAT'S ALL...
OH, YEAH, WHAT WAS THE NAME OF THAT BAND AGAIN?
UMMM... I FORGET... LEMME CHECK...

"MISOGYNISTS 'R' US"...
HMMMM... CHARMING...
Y'KNOW, LEONARD, I'M STILL LEAVING FOR NEW ORLEANS TOMORROW... YOU ARE AWARE OF THAT, AREN'T YOU?

HURRUMPH... YES, I'M "AWARE"... HOW CAN I FORGET?
AND YOU ALSO KNOW YOU CAN'T STAY HERE BECAUSE THE LEASE IS UP...
SO WHAT ARE YOU GONNA DO ABOUT A PLACE TO STAY? OR A JOB?...

BUT IF I PASS THE AUDITION I WON'T NEED A JOB! AND THEN EVERYTHING WILL FALL INTO PLACE...
WHAT'S THE MATTER, DON'T YOU HAVE ANY FAITH IN ME?
OF COURSE I DO, LEONARD, BUT "MISOGYNISTS 'R' US"? YEESH, I DUNNO...

THEN AGAIN, YOU COULD ALWAYS COME WITH ME, LEONARD...
PLEASE? PRETTY PLEASE WITH SUGAR ON TOP?
WHAT?!? AND GIVE UP ON NEW YORK? NEVER!!!
I'M EITHER GONNA MAKE IT BIG IN THIS TOWN OR DIE TRYIN'!

HELL, MAN, I AIN'T NO QUITTER!
ARE YOU SUGGESTING THAT I'M A LOSER?!? THAT I DON'T HAVE WHAT IT TAKES?!
OF COURSE NOT, LEONARD! IT'S JUST THAT...

—OH, FORGET IT! I'M GOING TO WORK!
I'LL SEE YOU LATER!

SLAM!

DIAL, DIAL, DIAL...

HELLO, ...ER... JAYNE?

HAT AFTERNOON...
HIYA, LEONARD! HOWZIT HANGIN'?
HUH? OH, HIYA, ANNETTE...
DOWNTOWN BERVIT
OPEN

HEY, WHY SO GLUM, CHUM?
OH, I'VE GOT AN AUDITION TODAY FOR AN OUTFIT THAT'S LOOKING FOR A DRUMMER, AND I'M PRETTY NERVOUS, SINCE I'VE NEVER PLAYED DRUMS BEFORE IN MY LIFE...

NERVOUS, HUH? I KNOW HOW THAT IS...
HEY, I GOT THE CURE FOR THAT! HOW ABOUT YOU 'N' ME GO OUT AN' GET WASTED!
NAH, I BETTER NOT. BESIDES, I'M BROKE...

'AY, THAT'S NO PROBLEM! IT'LL BE MY TREAT!
OKAY. LET'S GO!
JUMP!

.ATER...
...Y'KNOW, LEONARD, I ALWAYS WANTED TO BE A CREATIVE TYPE—A SINGER, A DANCER, AN AHTIST, WHATEVAH...
SSSSSSSSSUCK!

JUST TO BE ABLE TO MAKE A LIVING DOING SOMETHING THAT YOU LOVE—THAT'S THE LIFE FOR ME, I'M TELLIN' YA...
I HEAR YA TALKIN', "BAM-BAM"—IN FACT, I'VE BEEN THERE!
...DID I EVER TELL YOU ABOUT THE BAND I WAS IN?

ONLY ABOUT A MILLION TIMES...
...WE WERE CALLED "LEONARD AND THE LOVE GODS", AND MAN, WE TOTALLY KICKED ASS! PLUS WE WERE MAKING MONEY HAND OVER FIST!
WE WERE REALLY GOIN' PLACES, TIL OUR MANAGER WENT AND TOTALLY FUCKED US OVER!
THAT'S TOO BAD...
AAH, IT'S OKAY... I LOOK AT IT AS A LEARNING EXPERIENCE, SO'S I'LL KNOW WHAT TO LOOK OUT FOR THE NEXT TIME I...
—OMIGOD! I FORGOT ALL ABOUT MY AUDITION!
OH YEAH, THAT'S RIGHT— HEY, CAN I COME ALONG WITH YOU? I'LL GIVE YOU "MORAL SUPPORT"!
SLAP!
YEAH, SURE, BUT WE'D BETTER HURRY...
...I CAN'T AFFORD TO BLOW THIS CHANCE...
HUFF *PUFF*
ZIP!
ZOOP!
LATER...
OH NO! THEY'RE AN ALL-GIRL BAND! SHIT MAN, THIS SUCKS!
THEY SOUNDED LIKE GUYS ON THE PHONE...
OH, SO WHAT! YOU MIGHT AS WELL STICK IT OUT, AS LONG AS YOU'RE HERE...
WHICH ONE OF YOU IS HERE FOR THE AUDITION?
I AM, ONLY I'M NOT TOO SURE I, UH...
THAT IS, I...
RELAX, PAL. WE'RE "GENDER NEUTRAL" WHEN IT COMES TO HIRING...
SO, DIDJA BRING YOUR CHICKIE ALONG FOR "MORAL SUPPORT"?
I'M NOT HIS "CHICKIE", CHICKIE! AND WATCH YER FRIGGIN' MOUTH! IF THERE'S ONE THING I HATE IT'S A SMART MOUTH!
(PSST, ANNETTE! BE COOL, OR YOU'LL BLOW THIS WHOLE DEAL FOR ME)...
HEY, I'M COOL! SHE'S THE ONE THAT AIN'T BEIN' COOL, MS. SMART-MOUTH OVEH DEAH!
I'M JUST STANDIN' HEAH DOIN' NOTHIN'!

(OKAY, OKAY, YOU MADE YOUR POINT! NOW JUST BE COOL!)
I'M COOL! I'M COOL! BUT I SWEAH, IF SHE SO MUCH AS LOOKS AT ME FUNNY I'LL RIP HUH FUCKIN' FACE OFF!
SNICKER

TEN MINUTES LATER...
BLARE! BLARE! BLARE!

OKAY, HOLD UP A SEC...
I SAID HOLD IT...
CRASH!
SMASH!
BOOM!
BASH!

STOP!!!
HUH?
WHAT'S WRONG?

...WOULD IT BE TOO MUCH TO ASK YOU TO JUST KEEP THE BEAT FOR A CHANGE?
YEAH, WHAT'S WITH THE BUDDY RICH ROUTINE?
?!? WHADAYA TALKIN' ABOUT? I WAS KEEPING THE BEAT!

THIS IS PUNK ROCK WE'RE PLAYIN', ISN'T IT?! IF YOU'RE TOO LAME TO KEEP UP WITH ME THEN GET YERSELF A DRUM MACHINE!
I MEAN, JEEZUS!
HEY, ARE YOU SURE YOU'VE PLAYED DRUMS WITH A BAND BEFORE? BECAUSE I'M BEGINNING TO HAVE MY DOUBTS...

WHAT? I'VE ALREADY TOLD YOU I'VE PLAYED FOR LOTS OF PEOPLE!
I EVEN PLAYED FOR THE IG ONCE!
THE "IG"?
WHAT THE HECK IS AN "IG"?

I BEG YOUR PARDON! HAVEN'T YOU BROADS EVER HEARD OF THE GODFATHER OF PUNK?!?
?
'FRAID NOT, PARD'...
(PSSST! THIS GUY DOESN'T APPEAR TO BE TOO STABLE)...
TOOL

THE NEXT MORNING...

BUDDY BRADLEY
in
MY PAD
(REVISITED)
BY
PETER BAGGE
©1994
...OH BUD-DEE... GUESS WHA-AT...
WHAT?
THIS IS THE SONG THAT DOESN'T END...

...I FOUND US A NEW ROOM-MATE... *TEE-HEE!*
TITTER!
A ROOMMATE? BUT I—

HI, BUDDY...
YOU?!? BUT, BUT—

VALERIE JUST GOT ME A JOB AT THE SAME ESPRESSO JOINT SHE WORKS AT, SO I FIGURED WE OWED HER A FAVOR...
THAT'S RIGHT!
YEAH, BUT WHY—

WHY? BECAUSE THIS IS THE CHEAPEST LIVING ACCOMMODATIONS I COULD FIND, A FACTOR THAT'S VERY IMPORTANT TO ME AT THE MOMENT...
MIND IF I LOOK AROUND?
NO, BUT—
(PSST! BUDDY!...

...(CAN'T YOU SEE THAT SHE'S PERFECT? SHE'S HONEST, SHE'S RELIABLE, SHE'S EMPLOYED...
...(PLUS SHE'S CLEAN, WHICH IS A GOOD THING, SINCE WE'RE BOTH TOTAL SLOBS)...
(YEAH, BUT...)
EWWW, GROSS!
WIPE!

BUT WHAT?!
(BUT...I...UH...ALREADY FOUND US A NEW ROOMMATE TODAY)...
WEIRD...
SO THIS'LL BE MY ROOM, WHERE GEORGE USED TO LIVE?...

YOU DID?! WHY DIDN'T YOU TELL ME? WHO IS IT? DO I KNOW THIS PERSON?
WELL, IT'S...
WHAT'S ALL THIS JABBERIN' GOIN' ON OUT HERE?

...OH NO! NOT HIM!!!
I BEG YOUR PARDON! IS THERE SOME SORT OF A PROBLEM?
LISA, LET ME EXPAIN...

...(IT WASN'T LIKE I INVITED HIM TO MOVE IN OR ANYTHING! HE JUST SHOWED UP AT THE DOOR THIS MORNING WITH A SOB STORY ABOUT NOT HAVING A PLACE TO STAY.)...
(BUT WHAT ABOUT THE RENT? DOES HE HAVE ANY MONEY?)
HEY, WHAT'S THE BIG SECRET? ARE YOU GUYS TALKING ABOUT ME?

...(HE GAVE ME THIS $500.00 — DON'T ASK ME WHERE HE GOT IT FROM — SO HE'S COVERED FOR A FEW MONTHS, AT LEAST...
(AFTER THAT, WHO KNOWS)...
SAY, I'M GETTING PARANOID AS SHIT OVER HERE! IF I'M THE TOPIC OF YOUR DISCUSSION I'D LIKE TO BE IN ON IT!

THE PROBLEM IS THAT WE JUST RENTED GEORGE'S OLD ROOM TO SOMEONE ELSE, SO YOU'LL JUST HAVE TO FIND ANOTHER PLACE TO LIVE, STINKY...
HEY, NOW WAIT A MINUTE!

LISA, I ALREADY TOLD STINKY HE COULD STAY!
THAT'S RIGHT! FIRST COME, FIRST SERVE!

(BESIDES, I'M NOT TOO SURE I WANT HER LIVING HERE WITH US... IT'LL BE TOO WEIRD)...
HOW SO? YOU SAID YOU'VE TOTALLY GOTTEN OVER HER, RIGHT? RIGHT?!?
GOTTEN OVER WHO? NOW WHAT ARE YOU TWO TALKING ABOUT?
IS SOMEONE ELSE HERE? I HEAR A FAMILIAR VOICE...

...OH...IT'S YOU...

...WHAT IS THIS PERSON DOING HERE?!?
WELL, IT LOOKS LIKE WE'RE ALL GONNA BE ONE BIG HAPPY FAMILY...

LIKE HELL WE ARE! BESIDES, WHERE IS SHE GONNA SLEEP?
I SAY VAL GETS GEORGE'S OLD ROOM! YOU GET TO SLEEP IN THE PANTRY LIKE YOU USED TO!

FUCK THAT SHIT! THERE'S NO WAY I'M...
LOOK, WE'LL CUT YOUR RENT IN HALF IF YOU TAKE THE PANTRY...

...PLUS I THINK YOU OUGHT TO CONSIDER THE FACT THAT YOU REALLY DON'T HAVE ANY CHOICE IN THE MATTER...

...LIKE I SAID, WHO'S COMPLAINING?

THE NEXT DAY...
YO, BUD!
WUSSUP?
"BUCKET FOOD"
CHINA FIRST

YOU DON'T HAPPEN TO KNOW A GUY NAMED YAHTZI MURPHY, DO YOU?

SPLUT!

UH, YEAH, I KNOW HIM. WHY?
OH, IT'S NO BIG DEAL, BUT IF HE CALLS HERE LOOKING FOR ME, JUST MAKE LIKE YOU DON'T KNOW ME, OKAY?

BUT WHY WOULD HE BE LOOKING FOR YOU? WHAT DID YOU—
I HAD THESE ANIMAL TRANQUILIZERS THAT I WANTED TO UNLOAD DUE TO THEIR RATHER UNPLEASANT SIDE-EFFECTS, SO I SOLD 'EM TO YAHTZI BY TELLING HIM IT WAS SPEED.

OH NO! YOU DIDN'T! TELL ME YOU'RE ONLY KIDDING!
SWIG!
YEAH, IT WASN'T UNTIL LATER I FOUND OUT HE DOESN'T RESPOND TOO WELL TO BEING RIPPED-OFF, SO I'D RATHER HE DIDN'T KNOW WHERE I LIVE...

LOOK, STINKY, I'VE GOT MY OWN TROUBLES WITH YAHTZI MURPHY, SO THIS IS NOT WELCOME NEWS YOU'RE GIVING ME...
BUT LIKE I SAID IT'S NO BIG DEAL! HE MAY EVEN LIKE THAT STUFF I SOLD HIM! KNOWING HIM I WOULDN'T BE SURPRISED...
STILL, IF HE DOES CALL, PRETEND YOU NEVER HEARD OF ME, OKAY?
UGH... THIS KUNG PAO CHICKEN HAS A METALLIC TASTE TO IT ALL OF A SUDDEN...
CHINA FIRST

LATER...
...DUM DEE DUM DEE DOO...
THE POSIE'S "FAILURE"

WHOA!
DID I SEE WHAT I THOUGHT I JUST SAW?!

...VALERIE'S DOOR WAS WIDE OPEN, AND THERE SHE WAS, LYING ON THE BED WITH HER LEGS SPREAD, AND WITH NOTHIN' ON 'CEPT HER UNDERGARMENTS!
WAS THAT SUPPOSED TO BE A "SIGN"?
DOES THAT MEAN SHE "WANTS ME"?

WHOA NOW, WAIT A MINUTE, I BETTER NOT ACT TOO HASTY, 'CUZ WHAT IF I'M WRONG? WHAT IF I'M JUST IMAGINING THINGS?
THERE'D SURELY BE HELL TO PAY IF I ACT TOO PRESUMPTUOUS...

BUT WHAT IF I'M RIGHT? I COULD HAVE TWO "GIRLFRIENDS" UNDER THE SAME ROOF! THAT COULD BE GREAT!
IT COULD ALSO TURN INTO A NIGHTMARE, BUT... HELL, IT COULD ALSO BE GREAT!

I KNOW WHAT I'LL DO! I'LL STROLL RIGHT INTO HER ROOM IN AN INNOCENT AND NONCHALANT MANNER, AND HOW SHE REACTS WILL TELL ME ALL I NEED TO KNOW...

HEY, VAL? I —

EEEEEEK! GET OUT OF HERE! WHAT THE HELL IS WRONG WITH YOU?!?
THE FACE
FLING!

OH WELL...

THE NEXT DAY...
OH, BUDDY...
HURMPF...
...TONIGHT ON "HARD COPY".

...I'M SORRY IF I OVERREACTED WHEN YOU CAME INTO MY ROOM LAST NIGHT...
GRUNT...
GO AWAY AND LEAVE ME ALONE!

LOOK, I KNOW I MADE IT OBVIOUS THE LAST TIME WE MET THAT I STILL HAVE A "THING" FOR YOU...
BUT I ALSO MEANT IT WHEN I SAID I DIDN'T WANT TO CAUSE ANY TROUBLE BETWEEN YOU AND LISA...
...SO FOR AS LONG AS I'M LIVING HERE I THINK THAT YOU AND I HAD BETTER KEEP THINGS EXTRA COOL...
I KNOW, I KNOW... YOU DON'T HAVE TO EXPLAIN...
STAY TUNED FOR "THE SIMPSONS"...

NOW, LET ME GET THIS STRAIGHT...
?

...IF, LET'S SAY, LISA AND I WERE TO BREAK UP, OR AT LEAST COOLED OFF FOR A WHILE, YOU'D CONSIDER GETTING IT ON WITH ME AGAIN?
ER...WELL, I'D CONSIDER IT, YES...

BUT LOOK, I DON'T WANT TO BE THE CAUSE OF ANY BREAK-UP, SO IF YOU'RE PLANNING ON—
RELAX, NO MATTER WHAT HAPPENS BETWEEN ME AND LISA WON'T BE BECAUSE OF YOU...
SO DON'T SWEAT IT, OKAY?

YES, WELL, I HOPE NOT...

I'M GONNA TAKE A QUICK SHOWER. DO YOU NEED TO USE THE TOILET?
NAH.

SLAM!
HMMMM...

...THINGS HAVE BEEN STAGNATING BETWEEN ME AND LISA LATELY...
WE DON'T PORK NEARLY AS OFTEN AS WE USED TO...

PLUS LISA'S BEEN CHECKING OUT OTHER GUYS A LOT LATELY, SPECULATING ON THEIR DICK SIZES AND THINGS LIKE THAT...
SHE'S PROBABLY FEELING PRETTY RESTLESS AND ANTSY HERSELF THESE DAYS...
A TOTAL BREAKUP MIGHT BE A BIT TOO TRAUMATIC FOR THE TWO OF US RIGHT NOW, BUT WHO KNOWS? MAYBE AN "OPEN RELATIONSHIP" MIGHT BE THE TICKET...
THE IDEA SURE APPEALS TO ME, AND I WOULDN'T BE SURPRISED IF LISA'S THINKING THE SAME THING I AM RIGHT NOW...
SHE ALWAYS COULD READ MY MIND...

* SIGH *...

FUCK IT, MAN! I'M GONNA TALK TO LISA ABOUT THIS RIGHT NOW!
JUMP!
CLICK!

NOTHING VENTURED, NOTHING GAINED, I ALWAYS SAY...

HMMMM...

THEN AGAIN, SOME THINGS ARE BETTER LEFT UNSAID...
PERHAPS I OUGHT TO RETHINK THIS...

AWW, HELL! THERE'S NO POINT IN TURNING BACK NOW...
...LISA? ARE YOU BUSY?
WHAT DO YOU WANT?

WELL, I'VE BEEN THINKING ABOUT THE TWO OF US LATELY, AND I'VE COME TO THE CONCLUSION THAT...

YIKES!
GRRROWW!
LEAP!

LATER...
OH, VALERIE?
YES? I—

OH MY!
UHH, LISA AND I WERE JUST DISCUSSING OUR FUTURE TOGETHER...

...AND WE'VE DECIDED TO STICK IT OUT FOR A WHILE, IN SPITE OF WHAT DIFFERENCES MAY EXIST...
SAY NO MORE...
UGH!

WEEKS LATER...
WHAT THE HELL IS THIS!?!
CHOMP!

DID YOU SEE THIS? CAN YOU BELIEVE THIS SHIT?!?
WHAT IS IT?

IT'S A LIST OF NEW HOUSE-HOLD "RULES" I FOUND TAPED TO THE REFRIGERATOR DOOR BY THAT CLEAN-FREAK, EX-JIZ-JAR OF YOURS, MS. VALERIE RUSSO!
WAZZIT SAY?

WELL, AMONGST OTHER THINGS, IT SAYS THAT "ALL COUNTER AND TABLE SURFACES MUST BE WIPED CLEAN AFTER EVERY MEAL WITH SOAP AND WATER!
YEAH, WELL...
I MEAN, WHAT THE FUCK!?

AND GET THIS: "BOTH THE TOP AND BOTTOM OF THE TOILET SEAT SHOULD BE WIPED CLEAN OF ALL URINE TRACINGS."
WHAT THE HELL IS SHE TALKING ABOUT?!
I'M TALKING ABOUT YOU, LEONARD!

HUH? OH, HI, VALERIE... HEH-HEH...
YIKES!
BUDDY AND LISA ARE BAD ENOUGH, BUT I CANNOT BELIEVE WHAT AN INCONSIDERATE SLOB YOU ARE! YOU LITERALLY MAKE ME SICK!
RING! RING! RING!
UH-OH, PHONE'S RINGING...
GUESS I'LL ANSWER IT...

HELLO? OH, HIYA, GEORGE... HOW'S IT GOIN' WITH YOU?
AND WHAT'S THIS ABOUT ME BEING A "JIZ-JAR"?!?!? WHAT KIND OF THING IS THAT TO CALL A FELLOW HUMAN BEING?!?
NOW, NOW, IT'S JUST A FIGURE OF SPEECH...

NOT TOO GOOD, ACTUALLY. THE SITUATION BETWEEN ME AND WINIFRED HAS BECOME INTOLERABLE, SO I'M READY TO MOVE BACK...
MOVE BACK? TO WHERE? YOUR MOM'S?

MY MOM'S?! NO! BACK TO THE APARTMENT! I ASSUME MY OLD ROOM IS STILL AVAILABLE?
UHH... WELL...TO TELL YOU THE TRUTH... YOU REMEMBER VALERIE, DON'T YOU?
YOU PUT THOSE RULES BACK ON THE FRIDGE!
WHAT RULES? THESE RULES?
RRRRIP!

WHAT?!? YOU RENTED MY ROOM TO HER?!?
TELL HER TO GET HER OWN PLACE! OR BETTER YET, MAKE HER SLEEP IN THE PANTRY!
ER...WELL, STINKY'S LIVING IN THE PANTRY AT THE MOMENT...
POUND! POUND! POUND!
KICK! KICK! KICK!
LEONARD, GET OUT OF THAT PANTRY!
IN FACT, I WANT YOU OUT OF THIS APARTMENT RIGHT NOW!
NO WAY! I WAS HERE FIRST!

STINKY?! MY GOD, IT SOUNDS LIKE A ZOO OVER THERE!
MAYBE LIFE WITH WINIFRED ISN'T SO BAD AFTER ALL...
NOW HOLD ON A MINUTE, GEORGE! I THINK WE MIGHT BE ABLE TO WORK SOMETHING OUT...
SLAP!

"WORK SOMETHING OUT? WHAT? HOW?
JUST COME OVER WITH YOUR STUFF...I GUARANTEE THAT BY THE TIME YOU GET OVER HERE SOMEONE WILL HAVE MOVED OUT...
EITHER YOU LEAVE OR I'LL MOVE OUT!
FINE! LEAVE! AND DON'T STUMBLE ON YOUR WAY OUT THE DOOR, YOU...YOU...URINE TRACING!

THAT EVENING...
KNOCK! KNOCK!
SO, WHICH ONE OF THEM MOVED OUT?
OH, WELL, YOU SEE, I, UH...
HEY, GEORGE OLD PAL! LONG TIME NO SEE!
WHAT'S WITH THE SUITCASE? ARE YOU GOING ON VACATION?
HELLO, GEORGE...
?!?
N-NOW GEORGE, I CAN EXPLAIN EVERY-THING...
(YOU PROMISED ME THAT ONE OF THEM WOULD BE GONE!)
(I KNOW, I KNOW, BUT IN SPITE OF MY BEST EFFORTS THE TWO OF THEM HAVE PATCH-ED THINGS UP AND INSIST ON ACTING LIKE CIVILIZED HUMAN BEINGS!
(BUT DON'T WORRY, I'VE WORKED OUT A LONG-TERM PLAN...)
MORE HAZEL NUTS?
DON'T MIND IF I DO...
(NEVERMIND THE LONG-TERM! RIGHT NOW I'M TIRED, AND I WANT TO GO TO SLEEP—IN MY OWN ROOM!)
WHOA NOW, WAIT A MINUTE, GEORGE...
YOU! PACK YOUR BELONGINGS!! I'M MOVING BACK INTO MY OLD ROOM!!!
WHAT?!?
BUDDY! WHAT IS THE MEANING OF THIS?!
YEAH, IS GEORGE OFF HIS ROCKER OR WHAT?
HEY, WHAT IS GEORGE DOING HERE, AND WHY IS HE THROWING ALL OF VALERIE'S CLOTHES INTO THE HALLWAY?
I-YI-YI!

DID YOU TELL GEORGE HE COULD HAVE MY ROOM BACK? HOW DARE YOU!!!
YEAH, WHAT WERE YOU THINKING?
OKAY! ALRIGHT! HOLD IT!
NOW LISTEN UP: THIS WAS MY APARTMENT FIRST, RIGHT? I WAS HERE FIRST!
THEREFORE, I AM THE KING OF THIS HERE CASTLE, UNDERSTAND?
GRRRR... CRUMBLE..
I'M NOT TOO SURE ABOUT THAT...
NOW, I TOLD GEORGE HE COULD MOVE BACK BECAUSE HE NEEDED A PLACE TO STAY! PLUS HE'S THE ONLY TOLERABLE ROOMMATE I EVER HAD!
THE REST OF YOU ARE ALL DRIVING ME NUTS!
HEY NOW, WAIT A MINUTE...
I SAID YOU'RE DRIVING ME NUTS!!!
YIKES!
OKAY, YOU MADE YOUR POINT...
NOW, FORTUNATELY FOR YOU I'M WAY TOO NICE A GUY TO KICK ANYBODY OUT INTO THE COLD, BUT SOMEBODY'S GONNA HAVE TO SLEEP ON THE COUCH UNTIL WE DECIDE WHO'S MOVING OUT FOR GOOD...
SO, WHO'S IT GONNA BE, HMMM?
...WELL?!? WHO'S IT GONNA BE?!?

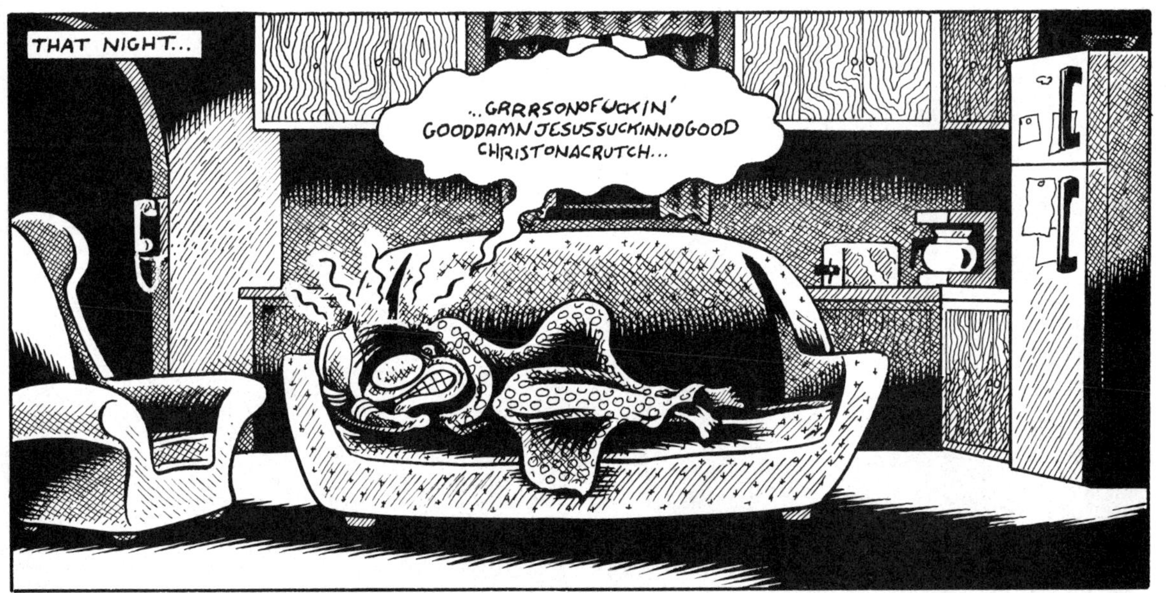

THAT NIGHT...
...GRRRSONOFUCKIN' GOODDAMNJESUSSUCKINNOGOOD CHRISTONACRUTCH...

...MAN, WHO WOULDA THOUGHT THAT LISA WOULD RATHER SLEEP WITH VAL THAN MAKE HER SLEEP ON THE COUCH...OR SLEEP WITH ME!
GODDAMN LESBOS...

...AND I LIKE THE WAY GEORGE STUCK UP FOR ME, TOO, AFTER ALL I'VE DONE FOR HIM...
HE JUST CLOSES THE DOOR TO HIS ROOM, HOOKS UP HIS COMPUTER, AND IT'S OFF TO PLANET GEORGE...
FUCKIN' INGRATE...

STINKY SHOULD BE THE ONE TO MOVE OUT, THOUGH...
I'LL BET HE'S SHOOTING UP RIGHT NOW...
NOTHING'S WORSE THAN A JUNKIE ROOMMATE...
TOO BAD HE'S PAID IN ADVANCE...

HELL, THEY SHOULD ALL MOVE OUT! EVERY LAST ONE OF 'EM— INCLUDING LISA!
IT REALLY BUGS ME THAT SHE DOESN'T SEEM TO CARE HOW INSANE THIS PLACE HAS BECOME...
"WHAT'S WRONG?" SHE KEEPS ASKING ME. "WHAT ARE YOU SO UPSET ABOUT?"
ARRRGH...

...SHIT, MAYBE I SHOULD MOVE OUT...
I'D DO IT IN A SECOND, TOO, IF ONLY I COULD AFFORD A PLACE OF MY OWN...

* SOB! *

A FEW DAYS LATER, AT SOME GROOVY HANGOUT...
PSST! HEY, BUDDY! C'MERE!
WUSSUP?

YOU DIDN'T HAPPEN TO SEE YAHTZY MURPHY ON YOUR WAY OVER HERE, DID YOU?
NO, THANK GOD...
WHY? NOW WHAT'S THE PROBLEM?

(SOMEONE JUST TOLD ME HE'S BEEN LOOKING FOR ME. I DON'T KNOW WHAT HE WANTS, BUT I'M SCARED SHITLESS)...
YEAH, WELL, IF THAT'S THE CASE I DON'T WANT TO BE SEEN WITH YOU...

NO, BUDDY, PLEASE DON'T GO! JUST SIT HERE AND CHAT WITH ME SO'S I CAN KEEP MY EYE ON THE DOOR...
THIS IS A WASTE OF TIME, STINKY, I'M TELLIN' YA...

WHY DON'T YOU JUST CONFRONT HIM? THAT'S WHAT I DID! BELIEVE ME, THAT GUY IS ALL TALK...
UH, YEAH, M-MAYBE YOU'RE RIGHT...

HEY, HOLD MY SEAT WHILE I GO TAKE A LEAK, OKAY?
I'LL BE BACK IN A SEC...
HUH? YEAH, ALL RIGHT...

WELL, WELL, WELL, IF IT ISN'T MR. BRADLEY...
?

OH! UH, H-HIYA, YAHTZI...
HAVE YOU SEEN LEONARD BROWN SLINKING AROUND THIS PLACE?

UHHHH... LEONARD WHO?
YEAH, YOU KNOW, THE GUY WITH THE ROUND SUNGLASSES AND FUNNY HAIRCUT? THE GUY YOU'VE KNOWN SINCE HIGH SCHOOL?..

...YOUR ROOM-MATE?
OHHHH... HIM. HEH-HEH! UH, NO, I HAVEN'T SEEN HIM LATELY...
W-WHY DO YOU ASK?

AAH, HE SOLD ME SOME SHIT THAT HE TOLD ME WAS SPEED...
WHAT-EVER IT WAS IT GAVE ME THE WORST HEAD-ACHE OF MY LIFE...
I SWEAR I THOUGHT I WAS GONNA DIE...

IN FACT, MY EARS ARE STILL BUZZING FROM THAT STUFF...
IT LEFT ME IN A FOG THAT I'M ONLY STARTING TO COME OUT OF...
YEESH...

YEAH. SO I JUST WANT TO TRACK HIM DOWN TO FIND OUT IF HE'S GOT ANYMORE OF THAT STUFF...
YEAH, WELL, I DON'T—
WHAT? DID YOU SAY YOU WANT MORE?

B-BUT, YOU JUST SAID IT MADE YOU FEEL LIKE YOU WERE GONNA DIE, AND THAT YOUR EARS—
I KNOW, I KNOW...

...BUT I LIKE FEELING THIS WAY...
?!?

OH, WELL IN THAT CASE HE'S HIDING IN THE MEN'S ROOM...
GREAT!

OH, AND BY THE WAY, BUDDY...
I LIKED THE WAY YOU NEARLY SHIT YOUR PANTS WHEN I WALKED OVER HERE JUST NOW...
OH...I... ER..,UH...

...AND IT SORTA MAKES ME LAUGH TO THINK OF HOW YOU FAKED YOUR WAY OUT OF TROUBLE THAT DAY YOU STOLE THOSE VIDEOS BY ACTING LIKE A PSYCHOPATH...
OH, SHIT!
B-B-BUT, I THOUGHT WE HAD AN UNDERSTANDING...

BULL-SHIT! ALL I UNDERSTAND IS THAT YOU STILL OWE ME $350.00!
THREE-HUNDRED AND FIFTY?!? FOR WHAT?!

THAT'S ROUGHLY THE RETAIL VALUE OF THOSE VIDEOS YOU DE-STROYED!
NOW, I'M WILLING TO GIVE YOU TWO WEEKS TO COME UP WITH THE DOUGH...
GULP!

...AND SHOULD YOU COME UP SHORT, THEN...
WHOA!
BAM!

HEH-HEH... I FAKED YOU OUT THAT TIME, DIDN'T I?
YEAH, HEH-HEH-HEH...

BASH!

HEH-HEH...

TWO WEEKS LATER...
EXIT
AHHHH... NOW THIS FEELS LIBERATING...

...IT'S GREAT TO GET AWAY FROM THAT MAD HOUSE I WAS LIVING IN, IF ONLY FOR A WHILE...
AND IT'S ESPECIALLY NICE TO GET AWAY FROM THAT BOOGIEMAN NAMED YAHTZI MURPHY...
JESUS...

PLUS IT'S ABOUT TIME I WENT BACK TO VISIT THE FOLKS, IF ONLY TO GET THIS FEELING OF OBLIGATION OFF MY BACK...

YESSIR, IT'S SUCH A RELIEF TO BE ABLE TO JUST WALK AWAY FROM EVERYTHING...
WELL, ALMOST EVERY-THING...

DID I MISS ANYTHING WHILE I WAS ON THE POTTY?
MISS ANYTHING? LIKE WHAT?

YOU KNOW, LIKE COFFEE, OR A SNACK OR SOMETHING...
OH...NO, NOT THAT I'M AWARE OF...

THAT'S GOOD. I WANT TO MAKE SURE I GET MY MONEY'S WORTH ON THIS FLIGHT...
THESE TICKETS WEREN'T CHEAP!

Y'KNOW, LISA, I HOPE YOU'RE NOT GETTING TOO EXCITED ABOUT THIS TRIP...
OH, BUT I AM EXCITED! WHY SHOULDN'T I BE? THIS IS THE FIRST TIME I'VE BEEN TO NEW YORK CITY! I CAN HARDLY WAIT!

BUT THAT'S JUST IT— WE WON'T BE STAYING IN THE CITY! MY FOLKS LIVE IN THE SUBURBS, WHICH ARE THE SAME AS THE SUBURBS EVERYWHERE...
YES, BUT WE'LL BE HANGING OUT IN THE CITY, RIGHT? AT LEAST SOME OF THE TIME, RIGHT?

WELL, YEAH, I SUPPOSE... BUT MY POINT IS THAT SHOULD WE DECIDE TO RELOCATE, WE'LL HAVE TO LIVE IN THE 'BURBS, AT LEAST AT FIRST...
I JUST WANT YOU TO KEEP THAT IN MIND, OKAY?...
OKAY, I WILL! SHEESH!

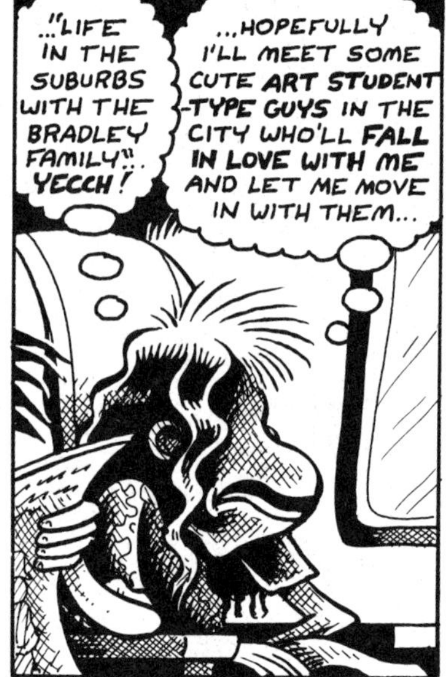

"LIFE IN THE SUBURBS WITH THE BRADLEY FAMILY" YECCH!
...HOPEFULLY I'LL MEET SOME CUTE ART STUDENT -TYPE GUYS IN THE CITY WHO'LL FALL IN LOVE WITH ME AND LET ME MOVE IN WITH THEM...

...THEN I'LL LAND A GLAMOROUS JOB AND GET MY OWN PLACE AND I'LL BE JUST LIKE MARLO THOMAS ON "THAT GIRL"...
AND THEN MY WHOLE LIFE UP UNTIL NOW WILL BECOME A DISTANT MEMORY, AND I'LL BE ABLE TO START OVER WITH A CLEAN SLATE!

I CAN'T BELIEVE I LET LISA TALK ME INTO TAKING HER ALONG WITH ME ON THIS TRIP!
...HOPEFULLY ONCE SHE GETS A TASTE OF MY FAMILY AND THE EAST COAST SHE'LL PANIC AND HIGHTAIL IT BACK TO SEATTLE!
IF THAT HAPPENS I'LL STAY BEHIND BY MYSELF AND START MY LIFE OVER WITH A CLEAN SLATE!

...LOVE ME, SWEETUMS?
OF COURSE I DO, SUGAR!
PAT PAT!
OY VEY!

RETURN TO HATE ISLAND!

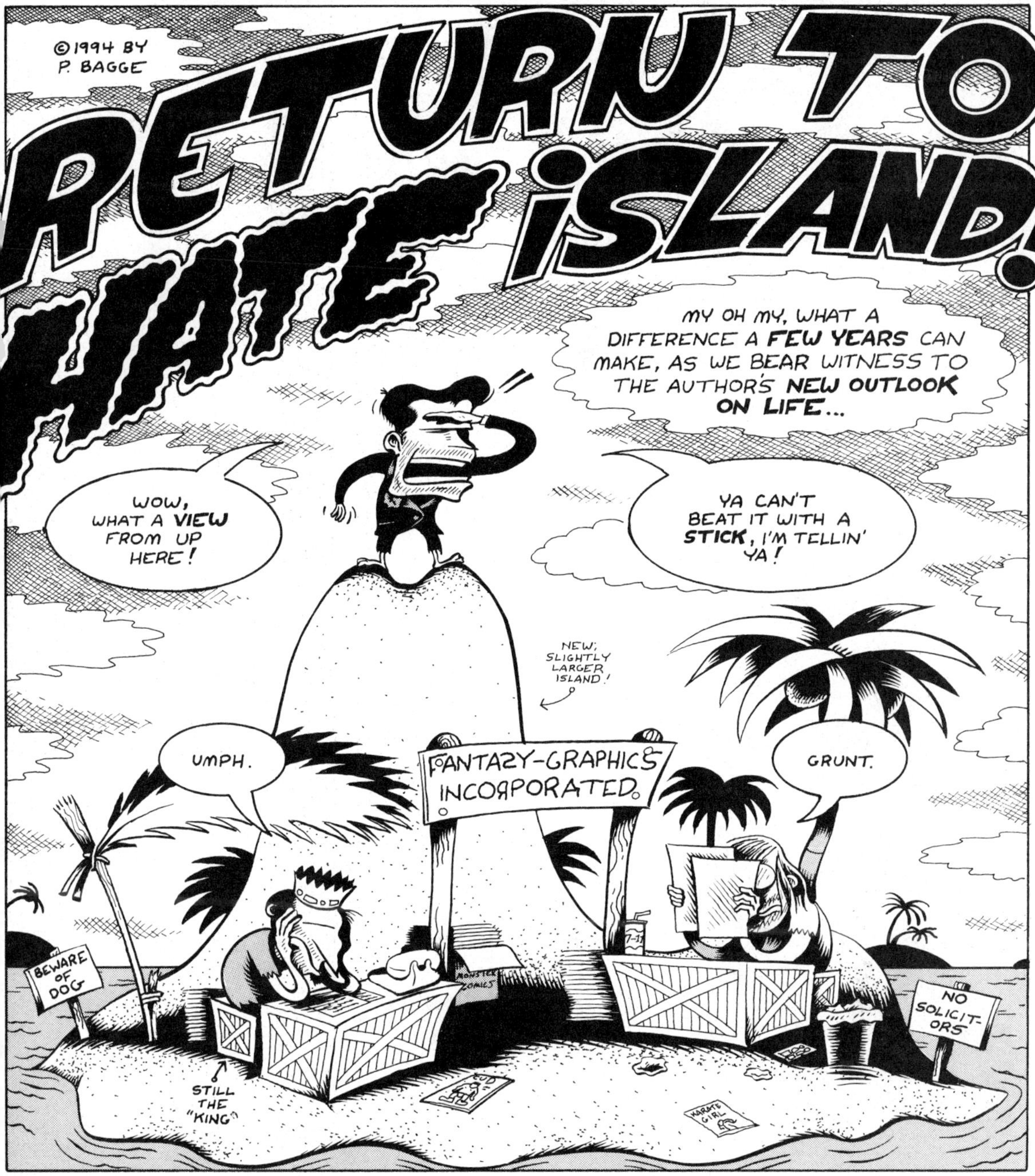

*I'M EXAGGERATING, SO PLEASE DON'T ASK ME FOR A LOAN.

WHAT? I'M DOING WHAT AGAIN?
YOU'RE RAINING ON MY PARADE, JUST LIKE YOU ALWAYS DO!
BEHIND EVERY DARK CLOUD LURKS MORE DARK CLOUDS— THAT'S YOUR MOTTO!
HATE

BUT THAT'S WHAT YOU USUALLY WILL FIND BEHIND A DARK CLOUD!
...LOOK PETE, DO WHAT YOU WANT! I'D JUST HATE TO SEE YOU BECOME A SELL-OUT...
BUT THAT IS WHAT I WANT!

SELLING OUT IS FUN!
SELLING OUT MEANS ONLY ONE THING— MAKING MORE MONEY!
THAT'S THE REAL REASON EVERYONE HATES A SELL-OUT! THEY'RE JEALOUS AND RESENTFUL!
BUT YOU DIDN'T USED TO FEEL THIS WAY...
UNDENIABLE FACT #1:
HATE
MONEY = FUN

THAT'S RIGHT! I USED TO BE A POOR SLOB WHO PUT GREAT VALUE IN SUCH NOTIONS AS SELF-RESPECT AND ARTISTIC INTEGRITY SINCE THAT'S PRETTY MUCH ALL I HAD AT THE TIME!
BUT NOW THAT I'M FINALLY EARNING A DECENT LIVING I'VE LEARNED A VERY VALUABLE LESSON: POVERTY SUCKS!
HATE

DO YOU HEAR ME? POVERTY SUCKS BIG TIME, AND I AIN'T NEVER GOIN' BACK!
DO YOU UNDERSTAND? NEVER! NEVER! NEVER!
OKAY! OKAY!
YOU MADE YOUR POINT!

...*SIGH*... I DON'T KNOW HOW I EVER LIVED WITHOUT MY HOME ENTERTAINMENT CENTER...
I THINK I'LL BUY ANOTHER ONE, JUST TO KEEP THIS ONE COMPANY...
BUYING AND OWNING THINGS IS SURELY THE GREATEST OF ALL PLEASURES...
HUMP! HUMP!
HATE

THAT'S WHY IT'S SO IMPORTANT TO ME TO KEEP GRINDING OUT "PRODUCT" AND SATURATING THE MARKET UNTIL PEOPLE ARE SICK TO DEATH OF ME!
SO COME ON, FELLAHS! GIMME SOME IDEAS!
HATE

UHHH... OKAY, HERE'S SOMETHING I'VE BEEN WORKING ON...
HOW ABOUT A PROMOTIONAL POSTER OF BUDDY BRADLEY IN HIS ROOM PLAYING A GUITAR, AND ON THE BOTTOM IT'LL SAY SOMETHING LIKE: "IF YOU LIKE TO GROOVE TO A DIFFERENT BEAT, THEN YOU'RE SURE TO DIG HATE COMICS AS WELL...
HATE

Panel 1:

Panel 2:

Panel 3:

Panel 4:

Panel 5:

Panel 6:

Panel 7:

Panel 8:

LET'S GIVE FASCISM A CHANCE!

WRITTEN BY AND STARRING
LAW-ABIDING CITIZEN AND TAX-PAYER
PETER C. BAGGE
© 1992

IT'S AMAZING HOW MUCH WORK IT TAKES JUST TO KEEP ONE OF THESE MODEST LITTLE HOMES LOOKING NICE...
...AND HOW EASY IT IS FOR SOMEBODY TO COME ALONG AND TOTALLY MESS IT UP...
GLUG GLUG...

THIS NEIGHBORHOOD IS DEFINITELY CHANGING FOR THE WORSE...ALL THESE SWEET OLD RETIREES NOW HAVE TO LIVE SIDE BY SIDE WITH THESE BOMBED OUT RENTALS FULL OF LOUD, OBNOXIOUS ASSHOLES...
...YOU NEVER USED TO SEE GRAFFITI OR BROKEN GLASS LYING AROUND WHEN WE FIRST MOVED HERE, BUT NOW IT'S A PERMANENT PART OF THE LANDSCAPE AND IT PISSES ME OFF...
CRASH!
TWEET! TWEET!
SQUEAL!
ANARCHY IN THE UH!
KILL THE RICH

...AND WHERE ARE ALL OF THESE HOMELESS PEOPLE COMING FROM? THE NEIGHBORHOOD'S FULL OF 'EM ALL OF A SUDDEN...
...IT'S LIKE THEY CAME BOILING UP FROM OUT OF THE SEWER OR SOMETHING...
FOOD GIANT
WILL STAND HERE ALL DAY FOR FOOD
I HAVE 28 KIDS
WILL SING BOB DYLAN SONGS BADLY FOR FOOD.
I WANNA PRETZEL, DADDY! PLEEEZE?
I WANNA PRETZEL TOO, DAD...

HEY THERE, LI'L GIRL! YOU'RE A CUTIE, YOU ARE! YOU'RE NOT AFRAID OF ME, ARE YA? CAN YOU SAY HI?
YIKES! BUM ALERT! BUM ALERT! GO AWAY! GO AWAY! TOUCH HER AND I'LL RIP YOUR SCABBY ARM OFF AND CRAM IT DOWN YOUR THROAT, YA DISGUSTING CREEP!
DON'T WALK
HI.
TOOT!
CLANG! CLANG!
WEEOOO! WEEOOO!
WARNING! WARNING!

HEY, PAL! CAN'T YA SPARE A QUARTER?
WALK
NO!
ZOOOM!
?

OH BROTHER, GET A LOAD OF THESE TWO TEENAGERS WITH THEIR "GANGSTA" OUTFITS ON
AND ISN'T TODAY A SCHOOLDAY? WHY DO I ALWAYS SEE SO MANY 14-YEAR-OLDS HANGING OUT AT ALL HOURS OF THE DAY?..
YO MAN, A DUDE WIT' A KNIFE BEATS A DUDE WIT' KUTCHA STICKS E'RY TAHM...
NO WAY, MAN!
TWINKLE TWINKLE LITTLE STAR...

WHEN I WAS A KID AND GOT OUT OF SCHOOL EARLY, EVERY ADULT I'D PASS WOULD SAY "WHY AREN'T YOU IN SCHOOL, YOUNG MAN?"
...IF I HAD THE NERVE TO SAY THE SAME THING TO THEM, THEY'D PROBABLY PULL OUT A GUN AND BLOW MY HEAD OFF!
JOSTLE! SHOVE!
TRY THAT AGAIN AND I'LL FUCK YOU UP — BIG TAHM!
WE'LL SEE ABOUT THAT, MAN!
ROW, ROW, ROW YOUR BOAT...

ber 23, 1992

Arson damages play e

By STEVEN SMITH, *Staff Writer*
and
RANDY BEAM, *Managing Editor*

Peter Bagge couldn't believe his eyes when he arrived at the Wallingford Playfield Monday morning with his 2-year-old daughter, Hannah.

Sitting on the end of huge playscape in the park were two pieces of wood that use to be part of deck of the playground equipment — the wood was ripped up by firefighters dousing an arson fire.

"We come out here twice a week and I was pretty shocked to see this," said Bagge, pointing to the hole in the playscape where the fire was set. "It took a while before I figured out what had happened. A lot of teen-agers and bums come out here to drink, so I wouldn't be surprised if one of them did this."

The fire at the Wallingford Playfield, at North 43rd Street and

Bakery manufacturing 12735 28th Ave. N.E. in L Sept. 14 and a fire Saturd that was set in grass and sh did about $1,500 in dama office building at 8001 S

Because of the rash of fires, businesses in nearly Seattle neighborhoods ha to take precautions.

A total of 943 arson been reported in Seattle start of the year, the n which were small fires garbage cans, dumpster rubbish, said Georg spokesperson for the Department. However bers includes 36 that h in the Greenwood neigh tween January and Au as the fires set in the la

"There has been an we're showing higher cause we changed system this year," "We're now recordi

WHEN IN ATHENS, GA., VISIT THE "BIZARRO WUXTRY" (225 COLLEGE AVE) IT'S THE FUNKIEST BUSINESS ESTABLISHMENT I'VE EVER SEEN!